The World of the
BIBLE
For Young Readers

The World of the BIBLE For Young Readers

by Yair Hoffman
Edited by Ilana Shamir

Viking Kestrel

How to Use this Book

The World of the Bible for Young Readers tells the story of the Jewish people and other nations in Eretz Yisrael (the Land of Israel) from around 2000 B.C.E.—almost 4000 years ago—to the 3rd century C.E. The initials B.C.E. are used to mark the years before the birth of Jesus. They are counted backward from the time of the birth, called the year 0 C.E. (Common Era). For example, when we say that something happened in the year 1000 B.C.E., we mean 1000 years before the birth of Jesus. If you add that number to the present year, you can see how long ago that was (for example, 1990 + 1000 = 2990 years ago.) The 18th century B.C.E. therefore includes the years between 1800 and 1700 B.C.E., and the 3rd century C.E. includes the years between 200 and 300 C.E.

This book can be read like a story from beginning to end, but chapters can also be read separately. Each chapter describes a particular time in Biblical history. The "boxes" in each chapter concern subjects that are related to that time, but are not part of the continuing story.

The book makes use of terms which refer specifically to events or concepts in the history of the Biblical world. These terms are generally explained in the text the first time they are used. An explanation also appears in the Glossary at the end of the book.

The language of the Hebrew Bible, known by non-Jews as the Old Testament, is Hebrew, so Hebrew terms are used here. They appear in two forms: as they are pronounced in Hebrew (such as Eretz Yisrael), or in English translation (such as the Land of Israel). The correct pronunciation of the Hebrew terms is given in the Glossary.

However, some Hebrew letters have no English equivalents. For example, "h," "ch," or "kh," may all stand for the same two Hebrew letters which are not exactly pronounced like any of these. These three different spellings are used because that is the way the words are traditionally spelled in English to approximate the guttural Hebrew sound. For the same reason, the Hebrew letter pronounced "tz" is sometimes represented by "z" alone.

Quotations from the Hebrew Bible are taken from the New Translation of The Holy Scriptures published by the Jewish Publication Society (1985). Quotations from the New Testament are taken from the King James version. The source of the quotation notes first the name of the book of the Bible, then the number of the chapter, and finally the number of the verse or verses; for example, Exodus 20:12-14 refers to a quotation from the Book of Exodus, chapter 20, verses 12 to 14.

The index at the end of the book tells you on which pages you can find information about the major periods, events, concepts and personalities covered in this book.

Translator: Sara Kitai
Design: Doreet Scharfstein
Proofreader: Ruth Lidor

Page one: Jerusalem, the center of the universe, on a map from the time of the Crusades.

Page two: A depiction of the Dead Sea, the Jordan River and Jerusalem encircled by its wall on the mosaic floor of a 6th century church in Medeba, Jordan.

VIKING KESTREL
Published by the Penguin Group
Viking Penguin Inc., 40 West 23rd Street, New York, New York 10010, U.S.A.
Penguin Books Ltd, 27 Wrights Lane, London W8 5TZ, England
Penguin Books Australia Ltd, Ringwood, Victoria, Australia
Penguin Books Canada Ltd, 2801 John Street, Markham, Ontario, Canada L3R 1B4
Penguin Books (N.Z.) Ltd, 182-190 Wairau Road, Auckland 10, New Zealand
Penguin Books Ltd, Registered Offices: Harmondsworth, Middlesex, England

First published in Israel by Massada Ltd. Publishers, 1989
First American edition published in 1989

1 2 3 4 5 6 7 8 9 10

Copyright © Massada Ltd. Publishers, 1989. All rights reserved

Grateful acknowledgment is made to The Jewish Publication Society for permission to reprint Biblical quotations from *Tanakh*.

Library of Congress Cataloging-in-Publication Data

Hoffman, Ya'ir.
The world of the Bible for young readers/Yair Hoffman, Ilana Shamir. — 1st American ed.
p.   cm.
Includes index.
Summary: A survey of the historical background of events and people that are mentioned in the Old and New Testament. Includes more than 300 photographs, maps, charts, and drawings as well as a time line and a glossary.
1. Bible—Juvenile literature.   [1. Bible.]   I. Shamir, Ilana.   II. Title.
BS539.H64 1989   ISBN 0-670-81739-2
220.9—dc19
                                                                    88-20832
                                                                    CIP

Printed in Israel by Peli Printing Works Ltd.

CONTENTS

Hieroglyphics are a decorative form of writing. Each picture represents one or more words or syllables.

The Egyptian "Book of the Dead," which was written in ceramic hieroglyphics on this wooden coffin 3000 years ago, consists of hymns of praise to the gods, who according to ancient tradition, helped the deceased in their afterlife.

INTRODUCTION: HISTORY AND LEGEND

This book tells the history of the nations and people who lived in Eretz Yisrael (the Land of Israel) for over two thousand years, during what is known as the Biblical Period. The story is accompanied by maps, diagrams, and photographs of places and sites, as well as of tools and other objects which were in use at the time the events took place.

Our story begins 3800 years ago in the 18th century B.C.E., and continues until the 3rd century C.E., 1600 years before our time. Historians who try to investigate what was happening that long ago in the United States, for example, soon learn they can find out very little. They even have trouble describing the life of the inhabitants of the country 1000 years ago. Who were their leaders? What were their religious beliefs? In the United States, the distant past is hidden in the darkness of the prehistoric age. But a great deal is known about what was happening during the same period in Greece and Rome, for instance, and in China, in Eretz Yisrael, and in Egypt.

Why do we know so much about some nations and so little about others? The answer, of course, is *writing.* The time when people began to write down their history (assuming some of these records have survived) marks the beginning of the historical period. The era before that, the time for which we have no written records of events, is called the prehistoric age—the time before history.

When the people of different nations began to write, they recorded more than just the events that occurred and the things they saw with their own eyes. They also wrote down the stories they had heard from their fathers and grandfathers, stories which had been passed down from one generation to the next for many, many years. They told of their ancestors, the men and women who lived before people learned to write.

These stories, which existed for so many generations before they were written down, are usually called *folk*

1. This Sumerian relief from the 3rd millennium B.C.E. depicts a ritual sacrifice. The marks around the figures are examples of ancient cuneiform writing.

1

2

3

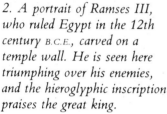
tales or legends. The question that bothers historians—the scholars who investigate the past—is how much weight should be given to them. Is every word in these stories true? Perhaps during the many generations in which they were passed from parent to child, from one family to another, and from one tribe to another, they lost some of their accuracy? It is only natural that when parents told their children about their ancestors, they chose to emphasize their heroism, goodness, and generosity, and ignored their bad qualities. They would also prefer to tell of the wars their ancestors won, and forget about the ones they lost.

Historians therefore distinguish between two sorts of written records: those which tell of things that happened during the prehistoric age; and those which tell of events which occurred at the time the records were actually written, or which are based on historic information—that is, on earlier written records of this sort.

Historians are indeed a little wary of folk tales. They take it for granted that such stories will contain miraculous events, exaggerations, and inaccuracies. Nevertheless, they try to find the historical truth within these

legends. How, then, do historians find out what really happened? Their job is very similar to that of a judge. They gather all the evidence, some of which is usually contradictory, and compare it and weigh the arguments until they arrive at what they believe is the truth.

The historians' evidence, therefore, consists of folk tales; written documents from the period they are investigating, such as the reports of kings, letters, law books, etc.; later documents which refer to the earlier period; and archeological discoveries. When all of these together form a logical picture, historians can assume that they have found the truth, or something close to it. On the other hand, if the evidence is contradictory, historians are faced with a problem. Who should they believe? To which piece of evidence should they give greater weight? Different historians might come up with very different answers to the same questions, just as two judges might not arrive at the same decision in court.

The Hebrew Bible gives the history of the Jewish people, and the New Testament tells of the early Christians —Jesus and his disciples. Some of these stories can be considered true

4

history; they were written at the time that the events they describe actually occurred. Some describe events that the author himself did not witness, and some are folk tales. The Bible is the most important religious book in the western world. Both Judaism and Christianity are based on the Bible, and the Moslems, too, accept its stories as the truth. For this reason, when historians disagree about certain historical facts of Biblical stories, it may be because they believe in different things. These beliefs may influence their decisions when the Bible contradicts other evidence available. And there are indeed other sources of historical evidence: the writings of the Egyptian, Mesopotamian, Persian, Greek, and Roman rulers; ancient scrolls; archeological finds; history books from the distant past which describe the events of the time during which they were written; and letters. These sometimes confirm the Biblical stories, sometimes add important information missing in them, and sometimes contradict the accounts in the Bible.

In this book, we have used all of these sources to describe the Biblical period in Eretz Yisrael.

THE BEGINNING OF WRITING

Writing first began to develop at about the same time in two different parts of the Fertile Crescent—in Sumer in the east, and in Egypt in the southwest. In both places, the basic concept was the same: if a person can say "sun" and everyone understands him, then he can draw a sun and preserve the word forever. And if that is the case, you do not even need a detailed drawing—a simple one will do. For example,

"sun" can be ● ●, ⊙ ⊘

and house can be ▯ ⊞ ▯ .

And what's this? ⋔⋔ ⋔ ⊔⊔⊔

Yes, a garden.

These signs were the beginning of the pictorial *hieroglyphic* alphabet of ancient Egypt. It was written on special paper made from the papyrus plant, which is where we got the word "paper."

Something very similar happened in Sumer, but the signs used here were different. The Sumerians wrote on soft clay tablets, making marks with a wedge-like tool. This is called *cuneiform* writing, and the signs all consist of different combinations of wedge shapes. For example, it is easy to see that the first sign below represents a head, and to understand how that drawing evolved into the cuneiform sign for "head":

The development of cuneiform writings from the 35th century to the 7th century B.C.E., is shown in the following chart:

Original c.3500 B.C.	Simplified c.3000 B.C.E.	Archaic Sumerian	Old Babylonian	Assyrian	Meaning
					Fish
					Ox
					God/heaven
					Sun/day/light
					To till/plow
					House

Gradually, the signs came to represent independent syllables, and many hundreds of signs evolved, since every language has hundreds of syllables. For this reason, the new form of writing which then appeared, alphabetic writing, was much better. Two types of alphabets also developed: one using cuneiform signs, and another using letters that were not formed by combining wedge-like shapes. This second kind of alphabet was also employed in the Land of Israel. The alphabet in which most European languages are written today developed out of the Greek and Latin writing which evolved from this ancient alphabet.

A ← ∀∀ḰKK
B ← 𐤁𐤁𐤁𐤁𐤁𐤁
D ← ◁ᐅ◁◁

5. Phonetic signs in Egyptian hieroglyphics (in Greek, hieros means "holy," and glyphein means "to carve"). The alphabet is made up of stylized pictures of real or mythological objects.
In the early 19th century the French scholar J.F. Champollion was able to read Egyptian hieroglyphics for the first time. This became possible when an officer in Napoleon's army found a stone on which an inscription was carved once in Greek, once in Egyptian hieroglyphics, and once in the Egyptian phonetic alphabet. The ancient inscriptions were written from right to left, left to right, or alternating between the two directions so that each line began directly below the end of the previous line. Some were even written vertically from top to bottom. It was only later that the Semitic languages came to be written invariably from right to left.

	ꜣw		wn		mr		ḥꜣ		šꜣ		tj
	ꜣb		wr		mḥ		ḫp		šw		tjw
	iw		wḏ		msꜥ		ḥn		šn		tm
	im		bꜣ,bk		nw		ḥr		šk		tꜣ
	im		bḥ,ḥw		nw		ḥs		zꜣ		ḏꜣ
	in		pꜣ		nb		ḥꜣ		šw		dr
	is		pr		nm		ḫt		vḏ		
	ꜥꜣ		mꜣ		nsꜥ		ḫꜣ		kꜣ		
	wꜣ		mj (mr)		nḏ		ḫn		gm		
	wp		mn		rw		sꜣ		ti		

6. Ancient Egyptian writing materials: an inkwell, thin reeds used for pens, and a papyrus scroll.

6

1 · ORIGINS

Our story begins in the 2nd millennium B.C.E. (a millennium equals 1,000 years), in the region of the Fertile Crescent. Two great civilizations developed here: Mesopotamia in the east and north; and Egypt in the west and south. Each of them grew up on the banks of mighty rivers—the Tigris and Euphrates in Mesopotamia, and the Nile in Egypt.

MESOPOTAMIA

Mesopotamia is Greek for "between two rivers." It occupied the fertile land between the Tigris and the

1. The Fertile Crescent—the area that stretched from desert to desert and included Mesopotamia, Syria, Eretz Yisrael, and Egypt.

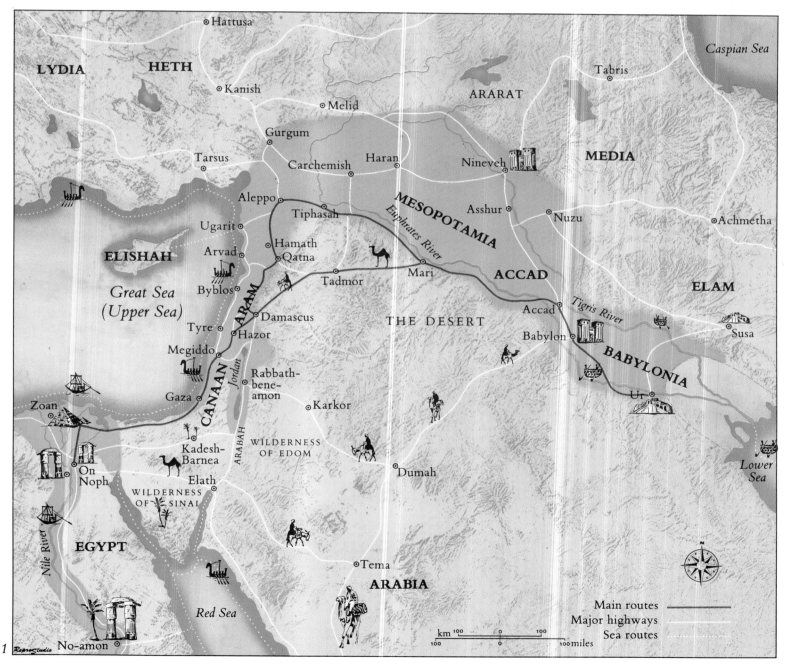

1 Reprostudio

2. A sketch reconstructing the ziggurat (temple) to Sin, the god of the moon, in the city of Ur. Babylonian tradition relates that the temple was built in the 22nd century B.C.E. The imposing structure, about 100 square meters (330 square feet) in area, is an ancient ziggurat, in the desert near the city of Susa.

3. Boats were the major means of transportation in ancient Egypt. This one appears in a fresco on the wall of a tomb from the 15th century B.C.E.

Euphrates, from the Persian Gulf in the south (today Iraq) to the Taurus Mountains in the north (today Syria). Several nations lived in the region in Biblical times: the Sumerians, Accadians, Babylonians, and Assyrians. They built majestic cities, such as Ur, Accad, Babylon, and Larsa. Sargon, the king of Accad and a formidable conqueror, ruled here, as did Hammurabi, the Babylonian king whose code of laws is one of the most ancient of which we are aware.

On the fertile plains between the

Tigris and the Euphrates, the inhabitants used the rivers to irrigate their crops, for fishing, and for travel and trade. In the large cities, temples were built to honor the most powerful gods such as Ashur, the god of the city of Ashur; Marduk, the father of the gods and god of the city of Babylon; Sin, the god of the moon and patron of the city of Ur; Enlil, the "managing director" whose temple stood in Nippur. According to Mesopotamian tradition, these and other gods, both great and small, controlled the world and determined the fate of people and nations.

EGYPT

Egypt in the southwest was also an important center of trade and culture. It grew up on the banks of the Nile, which provided abundant water for farming and fishing, as well as for travel. Here the pyramids were erected as burial places for the pharaohs, the kings of Egypt. To this day, we do not fully understand how the ancient Egyptians accomplished the great technical feat of building these pyramids. The hieroglyphic writing that developed in Egypt was used to record poems, stories, the annals of the kings, and innumerable

THE LAWS OF HAMMURABI

Hammurabi ruled in the city of Babylon in the second half of the 2nd millennium B.C.E., probably between the years 1792 and 1750 B.C.E. He is famous for the detailed legal code he devised, containing 282 separate laws which were to be followed when judging the people in his kingdom. The laws were discovered chiseled in cuneiform writing in the Accadian language on large stone tablets found in the city of Ur.

Here are three of Hammurabi's laws:

If a man accuses another man of murder, but cannot prove it, the accuser shall be put to death.

If a man commits robbery and is caught, he shall be put to death.

If a man knocks out a tooth of a man of his own rank, his own tooth shall be knocked out.

prayers to the Egyptian gods: Ptah, Osiris, Ra, Set, Horus, and Isis, to name only a few. The Egyptians believed that their many gods ruled the lives of the kings and inhabitants of Egypt both in this world and in the next.

THE PATRIARCHS IN CANAAN

Canaan, where Israel is today, was situated between these two great civilizations. It was a small country with no large rivers, and was mostly wilderness and mountains. Only a small part of the land was fertile plain. Some of the Canaanites were farmers, but most were goatherds or shepherds. There were no large majestic cities in Canaan. The people worshipped their local gods—El, Baal, and Asherah—in small temples and shrines. In the early part of the Biblical period, there were no great kings in Canaan either. Each city, and its nearby villages, were governed by a local ruler, and all of them were subject to the authority of the Egyptian king.

The first half of the 2nd millennium B.C.E. (the years 2000-1500 B.C.E.) was a time of great instability in Mesopotamia. Ur, the strongest kingdom in the region, was collapsing.

Tribes from the west, the Amuru, did not leave it in peace; finally they were victorious, and Ur fell into their hands. With Ur out of the way, other Mesopotamian kingdoms now gained in importance, those whose centers were the cities of Isin, Larsa, Babylon,

4. Abraham leading his son Isaac to the altar. This is part of the mosaic floor of the Bet Alfa synagogue from the 6th century C.E.

ABRAHAM'S MONOTHEISM

A legend written several hundred years after the Biblical period tries to explain how Abraham arrived at his belief in one god:

"When Abraham was three years old, he walked out of the cave, wondering: Who created the sky and the earth and me? All day he prayed to the sun. At night, the sun set in the west and the moon rose in the east. When he saw the moon and the stars around it, he said: That is who created the sky and the earth and me, and the stars are its ministers and servants. All night long he prayed to the moon. In the morning, the moon set in the west and the sun rose in the east. He said: They have no power. There is a master over them. To him shall I bow myself down and pray."

and Ashur. The Amuru tribes, who wandered with their tents and flocks throughout the Fertile Crescent, eventually conquered all of Mesopotamia. The family of Abraham, the patriarch of the Jewish nation, belonged to one of these nomadic Amuru tribes.

According to the Bible, Abraham's family first settled in Ur. From there they moved north to Haran, the city whose patron god was Sin, the god of the moon. It was in Haran that Abraham was commanded to leave everything behind him and take his family to Canaan—a strange land far

5. *The head of a pottery idol of the goddess Ashtoreth from the 11th century* B.C.E.

6. *These pottery idols show the gods playing musical instruments. They were found in Phoenician burial grounds from the 10th century* B.C.E.

7. *The god Baal was depicted as a warrior who smote his enemies with the club in his left hand and the lightning in his right. In this relief from the 13th-14th centuries* B.C.E., *the Ugarit king stands before him.*

8. *The routes followed by the patriarchs— Abraham, Isaac, and Jacob— as they wandered from place to place.*

from the major centers of civilization: "Go forth from your native land and from your father's house to the land that I will show you." (Genesis 12:1)

Why did Abraham obey this command? The Bible simply says that it came from God—not Sin the god of Ur, but YHWH, which means that Abraham believed in a single God. The Bible does not tell us what made Abraham start believing in one god—in monotheism—but merely states that he set out for Canaan— abandoning his nation, his relatives, his country, the land of his birth, and his tribe—because of his belief in one God.

When they reached Canaan, Abraham and his family wandered from place to place with their flocks. In this way, they came to know the land, as well as the people in it and their ways. They lived just outside the

cities, and did not associate much with the inhabitants of Canaan. The Bible tells of only one instance in which they bought land: in the Machpelah Cave in the city of Hebron, Abraham purchased a burial site for his family, affirming his eternal bond to his new land.

What was Abraham's status in this new land? This question illustrates the debate among historians as to the significance of the stories in Genesis, the first book of the Bible, that tell of Abraham and his family. Do these stories contain historical truth, or are they only folk legends which tell what a great man Abraham was?

From the stories in Genesis, we learn of the sort of life that Abraham's family led in Canaan. They wandered from place to place, seeking grazing land for their flocks and fighting with the local residents for the right to the little water there was. We are told that a real battle broke out with the residents of Shechem because of an assault upon Dinah, the daughter of Jacob.

When there was a particularly long drought, Abraham was forced to leave Canaan and take his family to Egypt. Because of the Nile River, Egypt was not entirely dependent on the rains for its water and so it suffered less from droughts. It was because of a severe drought in Canaan that later Jacob and his large family also went to Egypt. There they settled in a region where they could continue to raise goats and sheep, as they had in Canaan.

Why was Jacob's family allowed to settle in Egypt and why were they even given land for free? Genesis answers this question with the amazing story of Joseph and his brothers.

The Bible tells us that Jacob had twelve sons, but only two of them—Joseph and the youngest brother

SARAH AND HAGAR

The heroes of the Bible stories, even the greatest of them, such as the patriarchs and their wives, are not presented as ideal figures. They are human beings, and, like all of us, have very human emotions. Here, for example, is the story of Sarah, the wife of Abraham, and her maid, Hagar.

When Sarah was already advanced in age and still had not given birth, she decided to adopt a son. Following the custom for adoption that Sarah brought with her from Mesopotamia, she sent Hagar, her Egyptian maid, to Abraham so that she could have his son. This was the beginning of a bitter rivalry between the two women. Sarah felt, whether rightly or wrongly, that the maid did not show her the proper respect. She made Hagar's life miserable, until the Egyptian woman fled from her into the wilderness. There an angel appeared to her and told her to return, which she did. The angel assured Hagar that she would give birth to Abraham's son, and that he would father many children.

When Ishmael was born, he was officially considered Sarah's son, and not the child of his natural mother, Hagar. But this did not put an end to Hagar's suffering. Several years later, Sarah gave birth to Isaac, who immediately became the favorite son. In time, Sarah sent Hagar and Ishmael away into the wilderness, and told them never to return to Abraham's house. Hagar did not live to see the angel's promise come true, but the Bible tells us that Ishmael was to become the father of the Arab people.

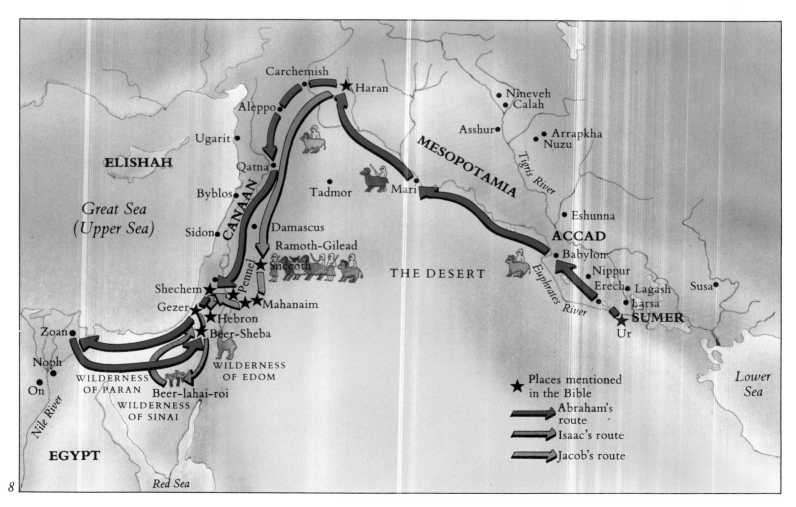

9. *A fresco on an Egyptian tomb from the 14th century* B.C.E. *showing the harvesting of the grain in Egypt.*

Benjamin—were the children of his favorite wife, Rachel. The ten older brothers wandered from place to place with the flocks, while the young Joseph sat at home dreaming great dreams. He dreamt, for example, that one day his brothers, and even his parents, would bow down to him. How was this dream answered? His jealous brothers sold him to slave traders, and he became a slave in Egypt.

After many years of bondage, Joseph was able to demonstrate his unusual talents and wisdom to the Egyptian Pharaoh. The Pharaoh was deeply disturbed by a dream he had. Joseph interpreted this dream for the Pharaoh to mean that Egypt was to suffer from a severe drought and even advised him how to prepare by

organizing his food supply more efficiently. Joseph's dream was coming true. He had won the confidence of the Pharaoh, and was put in charge of the Egyptian economy.

Again historians wonder if this story is historically true or merely a folk legend. Truth or invention? One thing is certain: it is one of the most dramatic stories ever told. And whether it really happened this way or not, the story shows the strong link between ancient Israel and Egypt. Interestingly, an ancient legend similar in many ways to this one was also found in Egypt.

So we see that the scene of the action in the Biblical period is the land of Canaan, situated between the two great civilizations of that time, Mesopotamia and Egypt.

2 · THE BEGINNINGS OF A NATION

Jacob and his family numbered around 70 people when they went to Egypt at the invitation of Joseph. In Egypt they grew into a large nation, and then left to find a land of their own.

Joseph was now the vizier of Egypt, which meant that his power was second only to the pharaoh, the Egyptian king. Some historians believe that the pharaoh under whom Joseph served was Amenophis IV, also known as Akhenaten (1367-1350 B.C.E.). He tried to convince the Egyptians to believe in one god—Aton, the sun god. Belief in one god was part of Joseph's faith, so Akhenaten may have gotten the idea from him. Other historians think that Joseph lived in Egypt one or two hundred years earlier, and that when Akhenaten became pharaoh he regarded Joseph's family—the Israelites—with favor. When Akhenaten died, Egypt returned to its traditional religion, belief in many gods. The Egyptian pharaohs now began to change their attitude toward the Israelites.

The Bible tells us of a new king in Egypt "who did not know Joseph" (Exodus 1:8), and he cruelly enslaved the Israelites. This may have been Rameses I or Rameses II (1290-1224 B.C.E.), but we do not have enough historical evidence to be sure.

What we do know is that the Israelites were put to work building cities and palatial structures. The Bible tells of the construction of two cities, Pithom and Ramses. Although the great Egyptian pyramids—which could not have been built without the work of tens of thousands of slaves

—were probably built before the Israelites were enslaved in Egypt, they give us some idea of the type of work they were made to do.

What was happening in the Fertile Crescent while the Israelites were living in Egypt, first in peace and comfort and later as slaves?

Between 1720 and 1570 B.C.E., Egypt was ruled by northern tribes called the Hyksos (the name means "foreign rulers"). The Egyptian kings managed to drive the Hyksos out of their

1. To build these pyramids at Giza, near Cairo, the Egyptian kings needed tens of thousands of workers for the construction and to transport the stones by boat from the quarries.

2. This caravan of men, women and children, whose appearance seems to be Semitic, is part of a fresco (wall painting) painted around 4000 years ago on the tomb of an Egyptian nobleman in Beni-hasan in Upper Egypt.

country. They now wished to make Egypt the strongest kingdom in the western Fertile Crescent. They launched many campaigns in the north, particularly against the mighty Hittite kingdom in Asia Minor (in the

3. Pharaoh Rameses III is shown conquering his enemies in this carving on a temple wall which sings the praises of the king.

4. Rameses III. His name appears on the right in hieroglyphics.

5. The pharaoh's overseers kept a close watch over the work in the fields.

region of Turkey today). To get to the north, they had to pass through Canaan, which suffered greatly from all these wars. In the year 1286 B.C.E., the army of Rameses II fought a major battle against the Hittites at Qadesh in Syria. Although the Egyptians were victorious, the Hittites were not totally destroyed. Peace treaties were signed between these two kingdoms in the year 1270 B.C.E.

Letters from the rulers of Canaan to Akhenaten were found at El Amarna in Egypt. From this ancient correspondence we learn that the Egyptian rule over the region was growing weaker. The small Canaanite cities which were subject to Egypt no longer feared to ally themselves with Egypt's enemies. One of these enemies is referred to as *Apiru* or *Habiru*. The letters reveal that the Habiru were tribes then settling in Canaan. They fought against the local rulers and even persuaded them to rebel against their masters, the Egyptians.

THE EXODUS FROM EGYPT

Although the Bible describes the Exodus of the Israelites from Egypt at great length, the event is not mentioned in any Egyptian document yet known. Neither is there any archeological evidence to support the Biblical tradition of a nation wandering for several decades in the desert, on its way from Egypt to Canaan. This is not surprising, however, since nomads in the desert do not usually leave evidence for archeologists to find because they do not build permanent settlements. Therefore, our only source of information about the release of the Israelites from bondage in Egypt and their journey to the Promised Land is the fascinating and highly detailed account in the Bible.

The hero of this story is one of the greatest leaders in the history of mankind—Moses. Moses appeared before pharaoh and demanded that he free the Israelites. The Bible tells us that when pharaoh refused, he and his nation were struck by harsh plagues until he finally had no choice but to allow the Israelites to go free. The Egyptian army chased after them, but according to the Bible all of the soldiers were drowned in the Red Sea after the Israelites had crossed the dry sea bed. These events, as well as the Israelites' journey from Egypt to Canaan and the miracles that happened on the way, are related in the Bible in great detail in the Books

WHERE IS MOUNT SINAI?

Despite the great importance of Mount Sinai in the Jewish tradition there is no evidence of its exact location. This is probably because the mountain was somewhere deep inside the wilderness, far from the inhabited land which the Israelites eventually reached and settled. It is also possible that the nation's leaders did not want the people to know where the mountain was, because they did not wish the mountain itself to become a holy place. The Jewish religion emphasizes the holiness of events themselves, not the place where they occurred.

Many attempts have been made to find the precise location of Mount Sinai. We know that it was a high mountain but there is more than one such mountain in the Sinai desert, and so there is still disagreement about just which one of them it was.

6

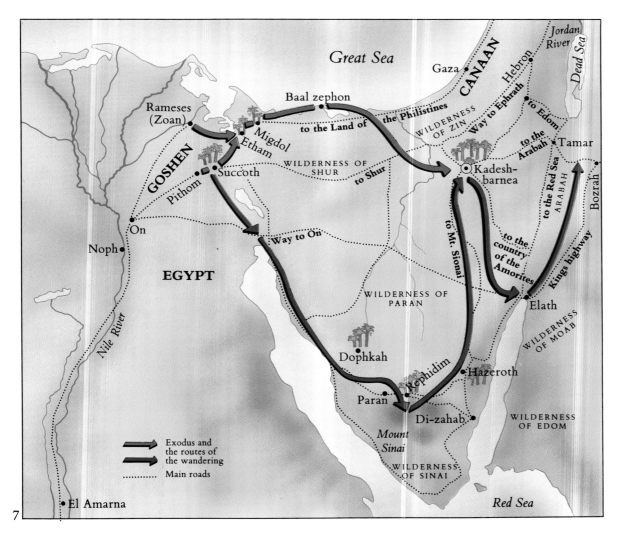

7

6. For about 1500 years, Jebel Musa, *the mountain of Moses, in the southern Sinai Peninsula has been traditionally identified with Mount Sinai.*

7. *The Exodus from Egypt and wandering in the wilderness.*

8. The Haggadah read on Passover tells the story of the Exodus from Egypt. Produced throughout the generations and all over the world, many of these books contain illustrations. In this illustration from a 15th century German Haggadah, God reveals Himself to the Israelites as they cross the Red Sea.

9. According to the Bible, the Egyptians suffered ten plagues —before Pharaoh agreed to let the Israelites leave Egypt. This illustration of the plagues, blood, frogs, and slaying of the firstborn comes from a 17th century Haggadah from Venice.

10. The Israelites departing from Egypt, as pictured by the painter of a mid-15th century Haggadah from Nuremberg, Germany.

of Exodus, chapters 1-19, and Numbers, chapters 10-13 and 20-25.

As we have seen, not all historians accept the Biblical account of the Exodus from Egypt as reliable evidence. However, all agree that these traditions help us to understand the nation that created them.

In the 40 years during which the Israelites wandered in the wilderness, these hundreds of thousands of freed slaves became a nation. At first, all they had in common was their memory of being slaves and a few tales of their ancestors in Canaan. The first and most important stage in their becoming a nation took place at the foot of Mount Sinai. Here God first revealed Himself and gave them a commandment which was to unite them as one people: "I the Lord am your God who brought you out of the land of Egypt, the house of bondage. You shall have no other gods beside Me" (Exodus 20:2-3). Thus the Israelites were now "The Chosen People," chosen to bear the burden of God's commandments, to hand down his message from one generation to another, and forbidden to be like all the other nations who believed in many gods.

In Exodus 20:12-14, other moral commandments were added to the belief in one God:
"Honor your father and your mother, that you may long endure on the land which the LORD your God is giving you.
You shall not murder.
You shall not commit adultery.
You shall not steal.
You shall not bear false witness against your neighbor.

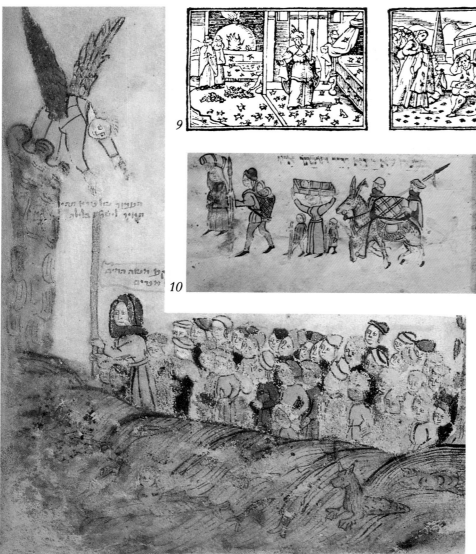

You shall not covet your neighbor's house: you shall not covet your neighbor's wife, or his male or female slave, or his ox, or his ass, or anything that is your neighbor's" (Ex. 21:12-14).

The Ten Commandments were the foundation of the nation's future legal system.

According to tradition, it was at Mount Sinai that the religious, national, and moral laws of the nation of Israel were established. Jewish law today is actually an interpretation

11

In 1887, hundreds of clay tablets were discovered at Tel El Amarna in Egypt, the site of Pharaoh Akhenaten's new capital. These were written in cuneiform in Akkadian. Some of them contained letters to the Egyptian king from the kings of the Canaanite cities who were subject to Egypt. Other tablets contained copies of the pharaoh's letters to these lands. These letters tell us about Egypt's status in the region during the 14th century B.C.E.

In one of the letters, the king of Jerusalem complains to the pharaoh about the kings of other cities in Canaan who were giving their support to the pharaoh's enemies, the *Habiru:* "To my master the king:...At the feet of my master I fall down seven times seven and seven times seven. Know all the things that concern my master the king....All of the lands of the king have agreed between them to war against me!...See you the city of Gezer, the city of Ashkelon, and the city of Lachish give them [the *Habiru*] food, oil, and all they lack,...so may the king send his archers against these people, for they have committed an offense against my master the king!...If there are no archers here, so will the lands and the rulers no longer be faithful to the king."

and extension of these ancient laws. A special holiday, Shavuot, commemorates the occasion and is also known as "the holiday of the giving of the Law."

The nation was put to the test in the wilderness. The Bible tells us of the people's complaints to Moses throughout the journey, of the lack of food and water, of the fear of attack from the desert tribes, and of the miracles God performed for His nation in the wilderness: He brought water out of a stone and provided them with quails for meat and sweet manna to eat.

The people's greatest test occurred when they drew near the Promised Land. Moses sent twelve spies, one from each tribe, to scout the land and bring back news of what they had seen. When they returned, ten of them reported that the nations in Canaan were too strong and could never be defeated. The people rose up against Moses, demanding that they return to Egypt! We can imagine the great disappointment of Moses and the few others who wanted more than

12

anything to settle at last in the land promised to them. The Bible tells us that Moses realized that the nation was not yet ready to enter its homeland. He understood that there was only one thing to do: wait—and lead them through the wilderness for 40 years until all of those who had been slaves would die. A new generation, born into freedom and

11. As the Israelites crossed the Sinai desert on their journey out of Egypt, they must have encountered water holes like these.

12. A desert oasis provides drinking water and the shade of palm trees.

Moses

Moses is undoubtedly the most impressive leader in the Bible. He is presented as a prophet who hears the words of God and brings them to the nation. He is a bold champion of freedom who fearlessly appears before the pharaoh and demands, "Let my people go!" He is a lawgiver who bestows on his nation a set of laws which serve as the basis of Jewish law to this very day. He leads his nation in war, guides it through the wilderness for 40 years under the most difficult conditions, and organizes an army that one day will conquer the Promised Land. And above all, he turns a group of unruly slaves into a nation. How many leaders in the entire history of mankind can compare with Moses as the Bible depicts him?

It is not surprising that there are many legends about this exceptional person. One of them tells of how Moses, as an infant, was thrown into the Nile in a small box, an ark, and was saved by the daughter of the pharaoh, who raised him in the royal court. It was only when he grew older and ventured out of the palace that he saw the injustice done to the slaves and realized that he too belonged to that enslaved nation. The brutality of the pharaoh's overseers enraged him. Finally, he killed one of them and had to flee from Egypt to Midian. There, while tending sheep, God revealed Himself to Moses in a burning bush. This happened at the foot of Mount Sinai, where God would later reveal Himself to the nation and give them the Law. God commanded Moses to begin the struggle to free the nation. This was the start of Moses's historical mission.

The most moving story told of Moses concerns his death. After the land to the east of the River Jordan was conquered and the people could now finally enter Canaan, God commanded Moses to climb to the top of Mount Nebo. From there he could look out over Canaan. God then declared: "This is the land of which I swore to Abraham, Isaac, and Jacob, 'I will give it to your offspring.' I have let you see it with your own eyes, but you shall not cross there." (Deuteronomy 34:4). Why? The Bible does not say.

For whatever reason, Moses did not live to enter the land of which he had dreamt for so long and for which he had wandered with the nation, preparing it for this moment, for more than 40 years.

13

unafraid of war, would then be ready to settle in Canaan.

And so, after 40 years of wandering in the wilderness, they arrived on the eastern bank of the Jordan River. Several nations lived here: the Edomites, Moabites, Ammonites, and Amorites. They had already begun to develop into independent kingdoms. Some of them allowed the Israelites to pass through their territory on their way to the Jordan River crossings which would bring them into Canaan. But other nations were hostile. The Israelites were forced to go into battle even before they reached the land promised to their forefathers Abraham, Isaac, and Jacob.

13. Moses in the ark, from a fresco on the wall of a 3rd century synagogue at Dura-Europos in Asia Minor (today Turkey).

14. The Tabernacle was a sort of portable temple used by the Israelites in the wilderness after the Exodus from Egypt. This painting is based on the description of the Tabernacle which appears in the Bible in Exodus 25. Note the cherubs woven into the rich cloth.

14

3 · THE ESTABLISHMENT OF THE ISRAELITE KINGDOM

The Book of Joshua contains the Biblical version of the conquest of Canaan by the Israelites. Once again, the Biblical account is highly detailed, while there is very little evidence from other sources. This raises serious problems for historians, who want to be certain about what really happened.

According to the Bible, the Israelite tribes camped opposite the city of Jericho. The spies sent out on a reconnaissance mission to Canaan reported that the people there greatly feared the Israelites. Joshua planned his campaign accordingly. He opened with an attack on the fortified city of Jericho, one of the oldest cities in the world. From there he went to the west and conquered the central mountainous region of the Land of Israel.

The Israelites gained more and more control over this important strategic region in the center of the country. Joshua now turned toward the southern coastal plain and conquered the principal cities in this area. The kings in the north joined

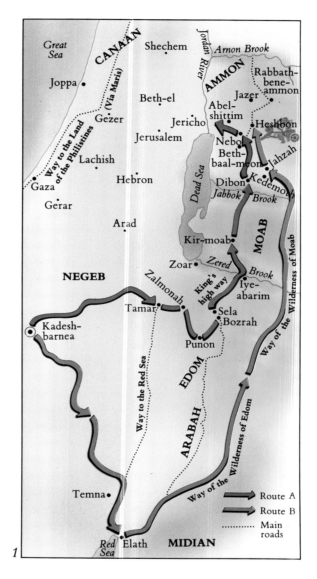

1

1. The coming of the Israelite tribes to the Land of Israel.
Route A: Earlier route through Edom and Moab.
Route B: Main later route bypassing Edom and Moab.

2. These scenes show Joshua the son of Nun and the Israelites conquering the Land of Israel. They are taken from a lithograph in a Venetian Haggadah from the early 17th century. On the left—the conquest of Sihon, king of the Amorites in Heshbon, and Og, king of Bashan (Numbers 21:21-35); on the right —circling the city of Jericho (Joshua 6:12-20); in the middle —the conquest of Ai (Joshua 6:1-29). The River Jordan runs through the center of the picture.

2

THE ESTABLISHMENT OF THE
ISRAELITE KINGDOM

forces to stop the Israelites. But Joshua's army was stronger. Hazor a major northern city, was conquered and destroyed.

The Book of Joshua tells us that these battles were accompanied by a series of miracles. The Israelites are described as a united and organized nation under a single leader. They defeated the entire population of Canaan in a rapid and well-planned campaign. However, not all historians are convinced that the whole nation took part in such an organized campaign. Some believe that the

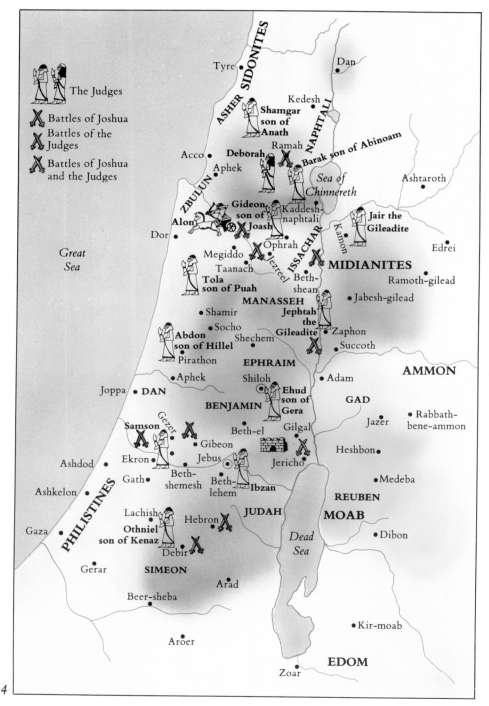

tribes came out of the desert in two waves and conquered Canaan. Others think that several tribes from the desert joined those Israelites who had never gone to Egypt, and together they overran Canaan. Still other historians believe that tribes from the desert entered Canaan little by little over a period of many years and fought sporadic battles. They speculate that it was only after more than 100 years that these tribes managed to gain control of most, but not all, of Canaan.

In spite of uncertainty about what really happened we can draw a

THE ESTABLISHMENT OF THE
ISRAELITE KINGDOM

general picture of the events from the Bible, in conjunction with the other sources available to us.

THE ISRAELITES SETTLE IN CANAAN

In the 13th century B.C.E., desert tribes entered Canaan. At least some of them had been slaves in Egypt. They may even have been welcomed by part of the local population, because they were related to them by race, language, and perhaps even family ties. The desert tribes, who were the seed from which the Israelite nation

6

grew, had their own religious traditions. These later developed into Judaism.

From ancient letters discovered at El Amarna in Egypt, we know that the kings of the Canaanite nations were attacked by tribes known as *Habiru* or *Apiru*. It is easy to see the similarity between these names and the word "Hebrew," a name sometimes used in the Bible for the Israelites. Some historians therefore believe that the invasion of the *Habiru* tribes in the 14th century B.C.E. marks the beginning of the entrance into Canaan by the Israelite tribes who had

been slaves in Egypt. More and more of these Israelites occupied Canaan during the 13th century B.C.E.

Another important source of evidence is a monument erected by the Egyptian king Merneptah in the year 1220 B.C.E. A poem boasting of the king's great victory is carved on the monument and the name "Israel" appears in it. Here is part of the poem: "The princes are prostrate, saying 'mercy.' Not one raises his head among the Nine Bows....Plundered is the Canaan with every evil. Carried off is Ashkelon; seized upon is Gezer;

3. (On page 24) One of the River Jordan crossings.

4. (On page 24) The judges who ruled the Israelite tribes before the establishment of the kingdom.

5. (On page 24) Jericho is situated near the River Jordan.

6. This statuette of a seated goddess in the shape of a chair comes from the Philistine city of Ashdod.

7. The economy of Israel at the time of the settlement.

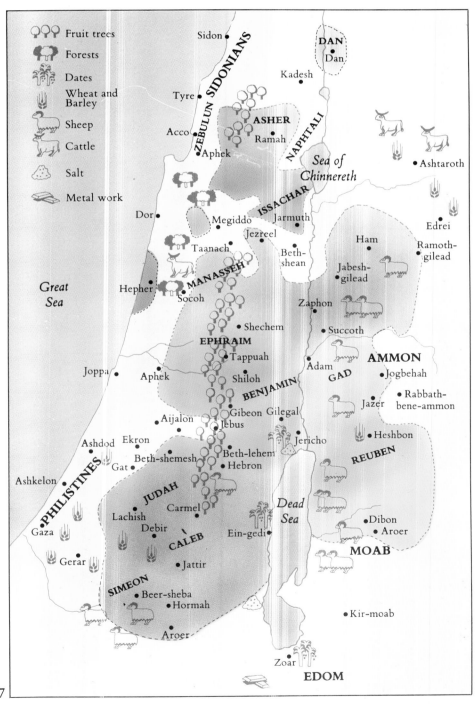

7

8

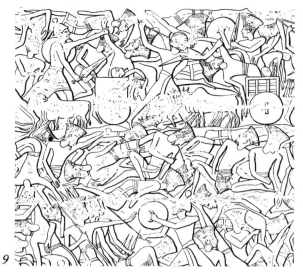

9

10

8. A wooden model of a Philistine boat, based on paintings and reliefs found on the walls of ancient palaces and tombs.

9. A scene from the land battle in which the army of Rameses III, king of Egypt, triumphed over the "Peoples of the Sea," among them the Philistines, in the 12th century B.C.E., the time of the settlement of the Israelite tribes. The painting is based on a relief paying tribute to the king which was found in an Egyptian temple. The Philistines can be identified by their feathered helmets and square chariots.

10. Pottery utensils more than 3,000 years old. They were found in a temple during the excavation of the ancient city of Lachish in the region of Judah. Note the figures of animals decorating the utensils.

Yanoan is made as that which does not exist; Israel is laid waste, his seed is not." This is the earliest non-Biblical record of the name. We can therefore be quite sure that there were already Israelites in Canaan at that time, although it is hard to say exactly at what stage their settlement then was.

Archeological evidence indicates that the 13th and 12th centuries B.C.E. were a period of destruction in Canaan. Signs of fire and ruin have been found in the ancient cities of Devir, Lachish, Hazor, and elsewhere.

All of this evidence, together with the Bible, points to the fact that during the 13th and 12th centuries B.C.E., a new nation began to form in Canaan—the nation of Israel.

The Israelite tribes were not the only people who were settling in Canaan at that time. As Egypt's control over Canaan grew weaker,

tribes from the islands of the Aegean Sea started to occupy the western part of the country along the coast. They were known as the "Peoples of the Sea." The Egyptian pharaoh Rameses III recorded on a monument he erected of a successful attempt to prevent one such invasion of Canaan in the year 1168 B.C.E. Actually, they were only partially successful. The "Peoples of the Sea" settled along the coast and became a very powerful nation—the Philistines.

The Philistines in the west and the nations to the east of the River Jordan—the Edomites, Moabites, and Ammonites—were a serious threat to the Israelites. This was especially true because the Israelites were divided into tribes. Each tribe was autonomous, and there was only a loose alliance between them. However, if one of the tribes was attacked, the neighboring ones would come to its aid. In addition, if one of the tribal chieftains was particularly strong and was accepted by the other tribes, he would become a sort of national leader. This period is known as the period of the Judges, because the chieftains served as the judges of their tribes. This was their principal function during times of peace. It was only at times of war that they also took on the role of military leaders.

The judge who was most successful in bridging the differences between the tribes and attaining the status of national leader was Samuel. He played an important role in the transition from a tribal society to a nation united under a king. There were two major reasons for Samuel's success. The first was his unique personality—he was universally respected for his integrity—which won him the trust of all the tribes. He was probably helped by the fact that he was not associated with any one tribe; he was a judge who wandered from place to place. The second reason is an external one—the

to understand the importance of national unity under a single ruler, people started to call for a king who would lead the nation after Samuel died. Despite the religious and social objections to a king, Samuel gave in to the will of the people.

KING SAUL

After a lengthy search, Samuel finally found a candidate for king—Saul from the Tribe of Benjamin. The Bible does not explain why a member of this tribe was chosen to be king,

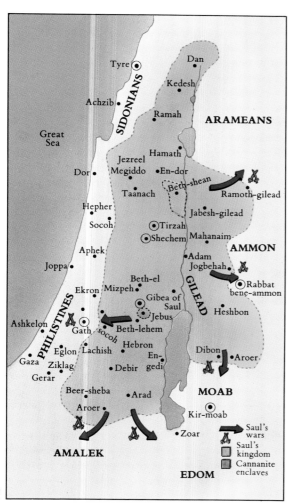

11

12

growing strength of the Philistines. The "Peoples of the Sea" now became a unified nation. They were not satisfied with their territory along the coast, and constantly tried to move eastward toward the Israelite settlements. In order to defeat this united power, the Israelites too had to join together. It was Samuel who symbolized this national unity. When Samuel got older, and the tribes began

but we may assume that the choice was not made by chance. The territory of the Tribe of Benjamin was situated between the strong southern tribes, led by the Tribe of Judah, and the northern ones, led by the Tribe of Ephraim. Benjamin was a small, weak tribe which was not allied with Judah any more than with Ephraim. Therefore, by choosing a king from Benjamin, it was possible to create a national unity that would overcome, if not entirely eliminate, the conflicts between the tribes that the transition to a kingdom might be expected to arouse.

11. Saul's war on the neighboring nations.

12. The prophet Samuel anointing David king (I Samuel 16:13), from a 3rd century C.E. synagogue at Dura-Europos in Asia Minor. The walls of this synagogue, one of the oldest ever found outside the Land of Israel, were covered with paintings of Biblical scenes. The building was discovered in 1932. The walls were dismantled and sent to Damascus, where the synagogue was re-erected inside a museum.

TRIBAL AND NATIONAL SOCIETIES

A tribe is a group of people—dozens, hundreds, thousands, or tens of thousands—who consider themselves members of the same family. Because of this, they are very loyal to each other. The tribe is led by a chieftain, who is assisted in running the tribe's affairs by people known as "elders." These functions usually pass from father to son. According to tribal traditions, the members of the tribe must submit to the authority of the chieftain and reject any other form of authority. Tribal loyalty makes the members responsible for each other. Vendettas, or blood feuds, are therefore a feature of almost any tribal society. If a member of one tribe kills someone from your tribe, then you must kill the murderer. The murderer's entire tribe is held responsible for what he did. This belief has led to many tribal wars, which sometimes last for decades.

By its very nature, tribal society is the opposite of a kingdom. The king does not wish to share his authority with the chieftains. What he wants is peace and national unity. To achieve this, he must allow the tribes less independence in matters of government, culture, and society. As a result, there are usually severe internal conflicts during the stage of transition from a tribal to a national society. Each tribe has its pride and a family tradition it is unwilling to give up. The chieftain does not want to turn his absolute power over to the king, and the elders do not want to be replaced by royal officials. When several tribes join together into a "nation" ruled by a king, it is only natural for each chieftain to demand that he—and nobody else—be that king.

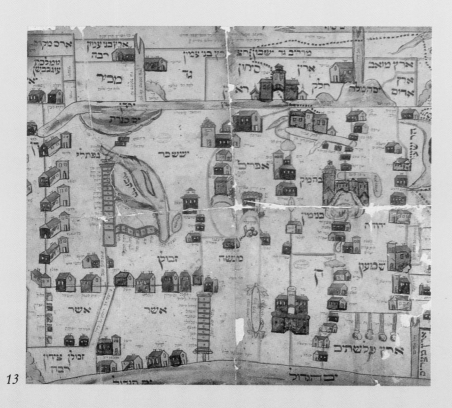

13

13. The Land of Israel, showing the territory of the Israelite tribes. This is a copy of a map drawn in the early 19th century by Rabbi Elijah, the Gaon of Vilna.

It was not long before Saul was put to the test. Nahash, the King of the Ammonites, attacked the Israelite town of Jabesh Gilead. The elders of the town petitioned Nahash for peace.

Nahash agreed on condition that he blind the right eye of each of the inhabitants as a sign of submission. The elders appealed to the new king, Saul, to save them.

Jabesh Gilead was situated in the northern section of the land east of the River Jordan, far away from the center of the country. The King of the Ammonites could never have imagined that men from tribes as distant as Benjamin, Ephraim and others, would come to the aid of the town. That is probably why he made such bloodthirsty demands of the townspeople. Saul, in a symbolic and dramatic gesture, called on all of the Israelite tribes to join him. He cut up two oxen and sent the pieces to each tribe, declaring that the same would be done to the oxen of anyone who did not join him in battle. The Ammonites were defeated and the threat was lifted from Jabesh Gilead.

Saul triumphed over Moab, Edom, and Aram, and fought numerous battles against the Philistines, the Israelites' most dangerous enemy. In many ways, Saul's leadership was different from that of the Judges. He alone decided which battles all the Israelite tribes would fight; he organized a standing army and appointed commanders to lead it; he rewarded his ministers with fields and vineyards, as was customary for the other kings in the region; and he established a royal court for himself with servants and slaves.

All of these changes, as well as the novelty of the kingship, put a terrible strain on Saul, and he was constantly in conflict with those who objected to what he did. His greatest opposition came from Samuel, because Saul gave himself authority over matters that had previously been in Samuel's hands, including the religious ritual, which had been the sole responsibility of Samuel as priest. His conflict with Samuel reached its peak when Samuel anointed the next king. Instead of choosing one of Saul's sons, he selected David, son of Jesse, the commander of Saul's army from the Tribe of Judah. The choice of David undermined Saul's mental stability. The final period of his reign was a tragic one. A disordered king tried in vain to pass his crown on to his sons. Nevertheless Saul established the foundations of a kingdom that continued to exist in Israel for more than four hundred years. His greatest achievement was military. The enemies threatening the Israelites on all sides were overpowered, and the Philistines, in particular, were now much weaker. Saul had spent much of his time warring against them. In one such battle in the Gilboa Mountains, around the year 1006 B.C.E., Saul and his sons were killed.

KINGS DAVID AND SOLOMON

When Saul died, the nation split into two camps. One camp, made up primarily of people from the Tribe of Judah, supported David, while the other camp, including Benjamin and the northern tribes, supported Ishboshet, the only one of Saul's sons who was not killed. This rift lasted for seven years. When Ishboshet was killed, David became king of all the Israelite tribes.

One of the first things David did was to choose a capital city to

14

14. "And Saul threw the spear, thinking to pin David to the wall" (I Samuel 18:11), from a painting by the 19th century French artist Gustave Dore.

15. Excavations of a site from the Biblical period near the wall of the Old City of Jerusalem. Seeking to uncover the secrets of its past, archeologists have been digging at various sites in Jerusalem, especially near where the Old City wall stands today. The wall in the background was built around the Temple Mount, near the holy Moslem mosque of El Aksa, after the Biblical period.

16. Part of a Canaanite ritual stand from the 10th century B.C.E., the time of King David's conquest of Jerusalem. It was discovered at the site of the City of David.

15

16

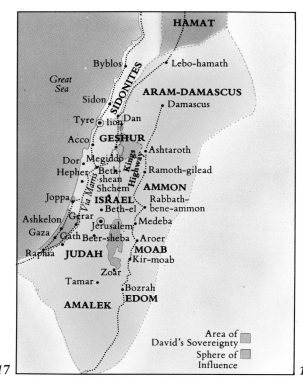

17

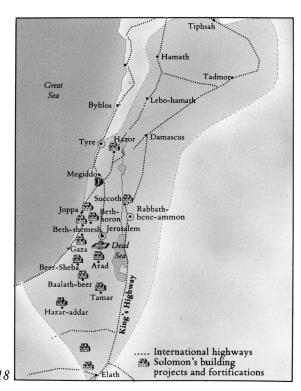

18

19

20

symbolize the nation's unity and help eliminate the rivalry between the tribes. He selected Jerusalem, which was situated on the border between his own tribe, Judah, and Saul's tribe, Benjamin. It was a well-fortified royal Canaanite city. If David could conquer it, he would gain prestige both among the Israelites and among the other nations in the region.

Jerusalem was indeed conquered around the year 1000 B.C.E., and David moved his court and the Ark of the Covenant there. According to tradition, the Ark of the Covenant contained the original tablets of the Ten Commandments, given by God to Moses on Mount Sinai. In this way, David began to establish Jerusalem as an administrative and religious center.

David completed what Saul had started and destroyed the Philistine enemy. He then defeated Edom, Moab, Ammon which were on the eastern side of the River Jordan, and Aram in the north, and turned these nations into subject peoples who paid tribute to Israel.

As David grew older, he no longer had to defeat enemies from without, but to put down rebellions from within. His son Absalom rose against him, and the northern tribes, who had never been happy with a king from the Tribe of Judah, also revolted. These were the first signs that the kingdom was breaking up, but it remained intact during the reign of David's son, Solomon.

Solomon became king around the year 970 B.C.E. He inherited a mighty kingdom, and it was his job to keep it that way. After decades of war during David's time, the country now needed a period of peace in which to build and to establish firm roots. Solomon achieved peace with the Egyptian pharaoh, whose daughter he married. He negotiated another pact with Hiram, King of Tyre, on the northwestern border of the kingdom.

In order to gain tighter control over his huge kingdom, Solomon divided the land into twelve administrative districts, and built and fortified cities in all of them. His greatest construction project was in Jerusalem. He enlarged the city, fortified it, and erected the royal palace and the magnificent Temple there.

Solomon's building projects were very expensive. To get the money he needed, he expanded foreign trade. He built a port at Elath, the southernmost point in his kingdom, and this served as the center for trade, which reached as far as Africa. But a large part of the income for the royal treasury came from heavy taxes which Solomon imposed on his people and on the nations subject to it.

Toward the end of Solomon's reign, revolts broke out in the subject nations of Edom and Aram. But the greatest threat came from within. The conflict between Judah and the northern tribes had begun long before, and now became even more violent, and Solomon, could not defuse it. The northern tribes, led by the largest tribe, Ephraim, felt they were not getting what they deserved. Finally, they openly rebelled, led by Jeroboam, son of Nebat.

21. *The Queen of Sheba visiting King Solomon, from a fresco in the San Francesco Church of Arezzo, near Florence, Italy, painted by the Renaissance artist Piero della Francesca. The figures are dressed in the style of the Italian Renaissance.*

22. *The Judgment of Solomon, a miniature from an illuminated 13th century manuscript.*

21

SOLOMON'S WISDOM

The Bible contains many stories demonstrating the great wisdom of King Solomon, for it is said: "The Lord endowed Solomon with wisdom and discernment in great measure, with understanding as vast as the sands on the seashore.... He was the wisest of all men" (I Kings 5:9-11). The Queen of Sheba "came to test him with hard questions," but "Solomon had answers for all her questions; there was nothing that the king did not know" (I Kings 10:1-3). One example of how wise a judge he was is the story of two women who gave birth at the same time. One of the infants died, and they both claimed to be the mother of the living child. Solomon ordered: "Cut the live child in two, and give half to one and half to the other." He knew the real mother would never allow this to be done, and thus he was able to identify her. She was the woman who protested his judgment.

22

4 · THE KINGDOMS OF ISRAEL AND JUDAH

1. The name of Ben-hadad, king of Aram, who waged war on the Israelite Kingdom, appears on this commemorative stone. It shows the Aramean god, Malkeret, holding a bow in his right hand and an axe in his left.

1

2. This diagram shows the wars between Israel and Judah after the kingdom was divided, and the attacks against them by Aram and Egypt.

3. A waterfall on the Ayun River, the northern border of the Kingdom of Israel.

The death of King Solomon, probably in the year 928 B.C.E., spelled the end of the united Israelite kingdom. His son, Rehoboam, lacked Solomon's wisdom and was unable to preserve the unity between the twelve tribes, some of whom had never fully accepted the rule of the House of David.

Jeroboam, son of Nebat from the Tribe of Ephraim, had fled to Egypt out of fear of Solomon. He now returned to Canaan and led the elders of his tribe, the largest tribe of them all, in demanding that the heavy taxes be lowered. Rehoboam's experienced advisors recommended giving in to the demands, but the new king ignored them. His response was arrogant: "My father flogged you with whips, but I will flog you with scorpions" (I Kings 12:11). The furious northern tribes took Jeroboam as their king, while the tribes of Judah and Benjamin remained loyal to Rehoboam. The Israelite kingdom was split in two.

The period between the death of Solomon and the fall of the kingdoms of Judah and Israel is described in the Bible in the books I Kings and II Kings. There are also Mesopotamian, Israelite, and Egyptian documents from this time in history. We

therefore have a fairly clear picture of at least some of the events.

RIVALRY BETWEEN THE KINGDOMS

Even though the two kingdoms shared the same religion and historical tradition, they were very different

3

from each other. Geographically, Judah in the south was mainly a kingdom of mountains and desert. Water was scarce and the people raised mostly grapes, olives, and goats. They had no outlet to the Mediterranean Sea because Philistine cities stood in the way. Their one seaport was Elath on the Red Sea in

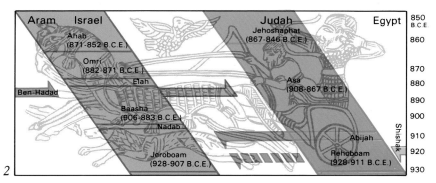

Aram	Israel		Judah		Egypt	
	Ahab (871-852 B.C.E.)		Jehoshaphat (867-846 B.C.E.)			850 B.C.E.
						860
	Omri (882-871 B.C.E.)					870
	Elah		Asa (908-867 B.C.E.)			880
Ben-Hadad						890
	Baasha (906-883 B.C.E.)					900
	Nadab					910
			Abijah		Shishak	910
			Rehoboam (928-911 B.C.E.)			920
2	Jeroboam (928-907 B.C.E.)					930

the south, but it could be reached only by a long and difficult route through the desert which was very vulnerable.

The northern kingdom was known as the kingdom of Israel, as Samaria (after its capital which was built later), or as Ephraim (after its largest tribe which had led the rebellion against the House of David). It was situated in a region of hills and valleys with plentiful water and a convenient outlet to the Mediterranean. In addition to grapes, olives, and goats, the people here could raise cattle, grains, fruits, and vegetables.

Strategically, however, Ephraim was less secure than Judah. The great Sinai desert separated Judah from the neighboring kingdom of Egypt, but the powerful states of Tyre and Aram bordered on Israel in the north and the east, and posed a constant threat.

Another important difference was that the inhabitants of Judah came from two tribes concentrated in a relatively small area. They also had a tradition of loyalty to the king. The ten tribes that made up the kingdom of Israel were spread out over a much larger area, and they continued to preserve their tribal traditions. When the new kingdom was established, they did not easily accept the central authority of the king. Thus, the House of David ruled in Judah for more than 400 years, but in Ephraim the dynasties changed in rapid succession. Nine different dynasties reigned in Ephraim in the 200 years of its existence! There were constant internal wars and rebellions, and the capital was moved from place to place. As a result, the kingdom grew weaker and weaker, and no national culture could develop.

Rehoboam could not accept the split in his kingdom. For a long time he fought against Jeroboam and the new kingdom of Israel. Most of the battles took place in the region of the Tribe of Benjamin, which marked the border between the mountains of Judah and the mountains of Ephraim.

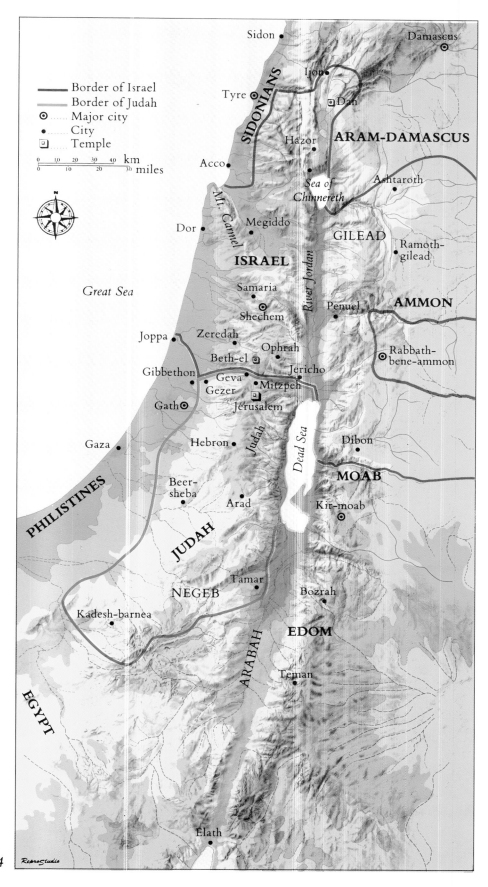

The war placed a heavy financial burden on Judah, because Rehoboam needed a lot of money to fortify the border with Jeroboam's kingdom. Since he was afraid that the neighboring nations would take advantage of the situation to attack

4. Note the differences between the two kingdoms on this physical map of Eretz Yisrael. Judah is mountainous with no outlet to the sea, while Israel has fertile valleys and plentiful water.

Jerusalem. To do that, he built magnificent shrines at Bethel near Jerusalem and at Dan in the north of his kingdom. Inside he placed golden statues of calves and declared: "This is your god, O Israel, who brought you up from the land of Egypt!" (I Kings 12:28). Thus religion also became a weapon in the political war.

Indeed, the Egyptians did take advantage of the internal war between the two sister kingdoms. For many years, they had not attacked the Israelites. The kingdom under David and Solomon had been too strong for them. But now the Egyptian pharaoh Shishak invaded, and overran both Judah and Israel. He erected commemorative tablets to his victories, listing dozens of towns in both kingdoms which his soldiers plundered, and telling of his threat to Jerusalem. In order to save Jerusalem, Rehoboam had to give Shishak some of the treasures of the Temple, including precious gold shields from the time of Solomon.

The rivalry between the two kingdoms Judah and Israel, continued during the reign of Rehoboam's

5. *The tunnel to the well at Megiddo, probably from the time of Ahab (8th century B.C.E.).*

6. *Tel Megiddo.*

7. *Tel Afek, a city located at an important crossroads in Judah. The walls were built in Crusader times.*

him as well, he also fortified the borders in the west, south and east, and this too was very expensive.

The war was not only fought for land, but also for the loyalty of the people. Jeroboam understood that he would have to create a new nation, and so he tried to disassociate the northern tribes from the Temple in successors. His son Abijah and grandson Asa also fought Jeroboam and his son, Nadab. Two years after Nadab became king of Israel, a rebellion against his rule, broke out. Nadab was assassinated by Baasha from the Tribe of Issachar, and Baasha proclaimed himself king.

Baasha signed a pact with Benhadad, the king of Aram Damascus, in order to secure his northeastern border. He was now free to renew the war against Judah. But Asa, the king of Judah, bought Benhadad's support with the remaining treasures of the Temple. Benhadad attacked Baasha and conquered large sections in the north of the kingdom of Israel. This—as we shall see—was not the only time that kings used the dishonorable idea of inviting a foreign nation to take part in a harmful internal conflict.

SISTER KINGDOMS

Aram's victories in the region (around 885 B.C.E.) convinced the leaders of the kingdom of Israel that their most dangerous enemy was Aram, and not Judah. So after many years of constant battles, the war between the two sister kingdoms came to an end. The threat of Aram and the growing strength of the nations in the eastern Transjordan sometimes even led the two kingdoms to join into a military alliance. To defend itself against Aram, Israel had to maintain a large army and to sign pacts with its other neighbors as well. This situation also influenced the religious and social life in Israel (see Chapter 5).

Large areas of the northern kingdom were conquered by Aram during the reign of Baasha until the northern kingdom fell in the year 721 B.C.E. This time the conqueror was not Aram but the great nation which followed it—Assyria. In Israel, Baasha's defeats led to internal rebellions and the rapid rise and fall of dynasties. In the four years after

Baasha's death, Israel was ruled one after the other by his son Elah, Elah's army commander Zimri who murdered Elah, Tibni who conspired against Zimri, and Omri who had fought against Zimri and was finally made king.

Omri reigned around the years 882-871 B.C.E. He understood that what the kingdom of Israel now needed was an end to war and time in which to grow stronger. He formed alliances with Judah in the south and with the kingdoms of Tyre and Sidon in the north. To secure these alliances, he had his daughter (some scholars say she was his granddaughter) Athaliah married to the king of Judah, and his son Ahab married Jezebel, the daughter of the king of Tyre.

In order to improve the economy of his kingdom, Omri imposed heavy

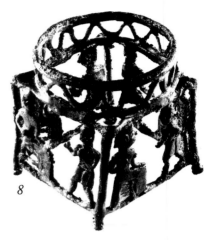

8

8. A bronze stand for a bowl from the time of the early kingdom.

9

taxes and increased his control over Moab in the east. A commemorative stone (called a *stela* in the Moabite language), carved in Canaanite-Hebrew letters, was found by a German clergyman in 1861 in the ancient city of Dibon on the east side of the Jordan. It was erected to commemorate Moab's victory over

9. Seals from the period of the kingdom. Stamped onto documents and property, they gave them legal authority or proved ownership. Most were engraved with figures or leaves, together with the owner's name.

35

capital, Samaria, was a prosperous city. There Ahab built himself a splendid palace.

The growing power of the kingdom was a thorn in the side of Aram. Again they decided to attack Israel. The Aramaean king placed a siege around Samaria, but he was defeated and forced to surrender to Ahab. According to the surrender terms, the Aramaeans had to return the towns they had conquered. Their king even

10. A view of Samaria, where King Omri built his capital: "Then he bought the hill of Samaria from Shemer....he built [a town] on the hill...and named [it] Samaria, after Shemer, the owner of the hill" (I Kings 16:24).

11. This stone railing for a window from the early 6th century B.C.E. was found in a lavish fortress near Jerusalem which was used by the kings of Judah.

12. An ivory ornament carved with the figure of the Egyptian child-god Hor seated on a lotus blossom. It was found during the excavation of Ahab's palace in Samaria, together with other ivory objects. Ivory, which had to be brought from neighboring countries, was a very precious material used to decorate furniture and other items. The many pieces found here indicate the great wealth of the royal house.

the Israeli conquerer who came after Omri. On it the Moabite king, Mesha, relates: "I am Mesha, son of Chemosh...king of Moab the Dibonite...and I dedicate this to Chemosh...for he saved me from all of the kings...Omri, king of Israel, who oppressed Moab for many years...and Omri held sway over the land of Medeba in his days and half of the days of his son forty years...." Thus Mesha's stela confirms that Moab had been subject to Israel during Omri's reign.

The policy of forming alliances helped to strengthen the kingdom of Israel and improve its economy. Archeological discoveries show that Omri began to rebuild and fortify the major cities of Megiddo and Hazor, although most of the work was apparently done during the reign of his son, Ahab. At the same time, Tyre was exerting an influence on the culture of Israel. Worship of Baal, the god of Tyre, became more and more popular, until it threatened to replace worship of the God of Israel.

Ahab (who reigned until 852 B.C.E.) enjoyed the fruits of his father's policies. During his rule, Ephraim became a strong kingdom and its

granted Ahab the rights to sell Israel's agricultural products in the markets of his capital, Damascus.

Ahab's victory over the Aramaean king was the first sign of a new development in the history of the ancient east: the growing power of the Assyrian Empire.

IN THE SHADOW OF ASSYRIA

In the year 835 B.C.E., the Assyrian king, Shalmaneser III, set out from his capital of Nineveh to conquer the kingdoms to the west along the coast of the Mediterranean Sea. In a stela commemorating his victories, Shalmaneser lists the armies that

13

14

15

joined forces to fight him: Aram Damascus, Hamath, Israel led by Ahab, Egypt, and others. Ahab's army seems to have been the largest in this alliance. A great battle was fought at Qarqar in the year 853 B.C.E., and it was probably won by the armies allied against Shalmaneser. Thus, they managed to hold off the conquest of the entire region by Assyria, but only for a few years. Ahab's pact with Aram did not last long after the battle at Qarqar. Only a year later, the king of Israel lost his life in battle fighting the Aramaeans.

While Omri and Ahab were reigning in Israel, Judah was ruled by Jehoshaphat, whose name means "God is the judge." He worked hard to strengthen both the political and the spiritual foundations of his kingdom. He increased control over Edom, improved the roads, and built up the fleet at Elath. He also reorganized the judicial system in Judah, appointing district judges and establishing a supreme court in Jerusalem. His special concern was to reenforce the faith in the God of Israel and the status of the Temple in Jerusalem.

After the death of Jehoshaphat, the kingdom of Judah joined a new alliance against Assyria. This time they were beaten (around the year 845 B.C.E.). Judah's enemies took advantage of the kingdom's defeat. In the east the Edomites rebelled, the Philistines invaded from the west, and tribes from the Arabian Desert in the south and the Syrian Desert in the north attacked. The kingdom of Israel was also vulnerable, and the Moabites freed themselves from its control, as their king, Mesha, tells on his stela.

More wars with Aram further weakened Israel, and again revolts broke out within the kingdom. The dynasty of Omri was overthrown by

13. Two Assyrian soldiers, one carrying a bow and the other arrows, on a 7th century B.C.E. relief from Ashurbanipal's palace in Nineveh.

14. This ornament from Ashurbanipal's palace in Nineveh shows the king going out to hunt.

15. Part of the memorial stone of Shalmaneser III, king of Assyria (8th century B.C.E.), showing Jehu, king of Israel, bowing before the Assyrian ruler. Behind him, Assyrian officials bear gifts.

Jehu, the rebellious commander of its army, who then became king. He was the first in a new dynasty which reigned in Samaria for about 100 years (from 841 B.C.E.).

The Aramaean threat to Israel resulted in the conquest of its lands in Transjordan and the destruction of many of its cities to the west of the River Jordan. By the time Jehu's son, Jehoahaz, took power, his kingdom consisted only of the area around the city of Samaria.

Samaria's position began to improve when Adadnirari III became king of Assyria. He fought the

kingdoms in the west and defeated Aram. Thus Jehoahaz was able to free Israel from subjection to Aram and to rebuild his kingdom. He reconquered large areas in the north and in eastern Transjordan, and even attacked Amaziah, the king of Judah, in Jerusalem.

When this new war between Judah and Israel finally ended, a period of economic prosperity and military strength began for the two sister kingdoms. Jeroboam II, the son of Jehoash, was now king of Israel, and Uzziah reigned in Judah. Jeroboam II made Israel the largest kingdom it had been since its establishment by Jeroboam I more than 150 years before. Uzziah expanded the territory of the kingdom of Judah, developed its agriculture in the south, built fortified cities, conquered Edom, and reopened the port at Elath. With this great prosperity, the rich lived in luxury, corruption was rife, and the poorer classes were badly exploited.

16

16. King Ashurbanipal celebrates a victory in the palace courtyard amid grapevines and date palms. His servants bring him food and wine, play music, and fan him with palm leaves. The relief was found in the king's palace in Nineveh.

17. A battering ram used by the Assyrians to topple the walls of the cities they besieged appears on this relief from Ashurbanipal's palace in Nineveh. The most common weapons of war at the time were bows and arrows.

17

The End of the Kingdom of Israel

During the approximately 20 years between the death of Jeroboam II and the fall of the kingdom of Israel in 721 B.C.E., no fewer than six different kings ruled Samaria. Four of them assumed power by overthrowing the previous king.

Fearing Assyria, Pekah, king of Israel, formed an alliance with Rezin, king of Aram. In the year 734 B.C.E., Pekah and Rezin threatened to attack Jerusalem, if the king of Judah, Ahaz, the grandson of Uzziah, did not join their alliance. Ahaz refused, and this is probably what saved Jerusalem from the fate that awaited Samaria. Tiglath-Pileser III, king of Assyria, conquered and destroyed Aram Damascus, and then conquered the northern regions of the kingdom of Israel. He made this territory part of the Assyrian Empire and sent its citizens into exile in other lands.

Tiglath-Pileser III died in 727 B.C.E., and the new king of Assyria was now

18

Shalmaneser V. The people in what was left of the kingdom of Israel hoped that the death of the Assyrian king would weaken their enemy. Encouraged by Egypt, a movement to revolt gained momentum in Israel and the neighboring nations. Hoshea, son of Elah, king of Israel, was convinced that he could free himself from Assyrian control, so he rebelled. The Assyrians responded by placing a siege around Samaria. The city fell to the Assyrian king, Sargon II, in the year 721 B.C.E.

This was not only the end of the kingdom of Israel, but also the end of the existence of its tribes as a nation. In order to destroy its enemies completely, Assyria deported many of the inhabitants of the nations it conquered. Tens of thousands of people from the kingdom of Israel were exiled from their land and scattered throughout the Assyrian

19

18. The people of Lachish going into exile with whatever possessions they can carry on their backs, on a relief from the palace of Sennacherib, king of Assyria.

19. The kingdoms of Israel and Judah at the time of Uzziah and Jeroboam II.

20. A letter on a clay tablet sent from Lachish shortly before the city fell to Babylon.

20

21. The ruins of fortifications from the period of the kingdom were found at Ein Gedi by the Dead Sea. They were used to defend the road from the desert plain to the Judean Hills and Jerusalem.

22. Hezekiah's Pool in Jerusalem, in a 19th century photograph.

23. Most of the inhabitants of Eretz Yisrael were farmers. This 19th century flour mill was patterned after the ones used in ancient times.

empire. As time passed, they lost their national identity. In their stead, exiles from other nations in the empire were settled in Israel. These people shared no common religion or history. Later, however, these new inhabitants of the land, as well as some Israelites who had been allowed to remain, adopted a large part of the principles of the religion of Israel, and became a new nation—the Samaritans.

THE KINGDOM OF JUDAH STANDS ALONE

The kingdom of Judah was left on its own. Its king, Hezekiah, fought hard

politically and militarily to prevent Judah from falling into the hands of Assyria. He formed alliances with the other kings in the region, and together they planned to rise up against Assyria when the time was ripe. He fortified Jerusalem so that it could withstand a siege. One of his projects in particular shows great engineering skill. A tunnel was dug from Jerusalem to the underground Siloam Pool beyond the city walls in order to ensure the city's water supply even during a siege. Two groups of workmen dug this tunnel, each starting at the opposite end. The joy they felt when they met in the middle is expressed in a Hebrew inscription carved in the wall. It was found in 1880 and today is in the Museum of the Ancient East in Istanbul. It reads in part: "While there were still three cubits to be cut through [there was heard] the voice of a man calling to his fellow for there was overlap in the rock on the right. ...And when the tunnel was driven through, the quarrymen hewed [the rock] each man toward his fellow, axe against axe, and the water flowed from the spring toward the reservoir for 1200 cubits and the height of the rock above the heads of the quarrymen was 100 cubits."

In the year 701 B.C.E., Sennacherib,

21

22

23

the king of Assyria, attacked Judah. He conquered and destroyed dozens of fortified cities and villages. He commemorated his victory over one of these cities, Lachish, in a lavish relief carved in his royal palace. As feared, he placed Jerusalem under siege and almost captured the city.

idol worship existed side by side with worship of the God of Israel.

THE RISE OF BABYLON

In the last quarter of the 7th century B.C.E. (2600 years ago), the city of Babylon grew stronger. The Chaldeans who lived in this ancient city rebelled against Assyria. They were aided by other nations, primarily the Medes. They now became an important force in Mesopotamia. As a result, the Assyrian hold over Judah was weakened, and the king of Judah, Josiah, used the opportunity to build up his kingdom. He wiped out the

24. The steps to the Gihon Spring from which water was channeled to Hezekiah's Pool inside the city.

25. The Israelites were exiled to Assyria (701 B.C.E.), and peoples from the Assyrian Empire were settled in Eretz Yisrael.

26. Most of the utensils in the Biblical period were made of clay. These jugs and plates were found near Jerusalem.

27. (On page 42) Reproduction of a plow from the Biblical period.

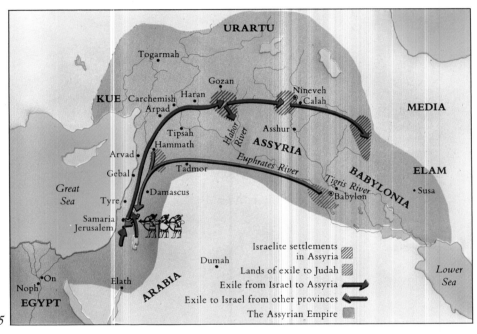

But for some reason we do not know, he suddenly lifted the siege and returned to his own country. There are different explanations for this in the Bible and in Assyrian documents, so we cannot be sure what really happened. It is clear, however, that Jerusalem was saved, just as the Prophet Isaiah had promised Hezekiah it would be. Nevertheless, Judah was now subject to Assyria and had to pay heavy taxes to it for many years. Assyrian culture and religion also influenced the kingdom. After the death of Hezekiah, Assyrian idol worship even invaded the Temple itself; and in all of the cities of Judah,

27

28

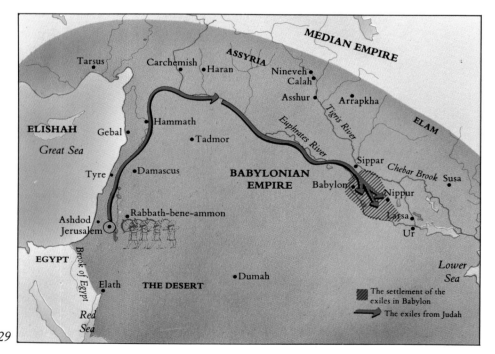

29

28. *This fresco from an Egyptian tomb shows how wheat was plowed and reaped.*

29. *The Babylonian exile.*

pagan rites, purified the Temple, called on the Israelites—the remnants of the Samarian kingdom—to unite under the rule of the House of David, and expanded his territory to the east and the west.

The balance of power was changing in the region of the Fertile Crescent. Egypt, for many years the rival of Assyria, now became an ally of its former enemy. Together they tried to hold back the Babylonians. In 609 B.C.E., the Egyptian king, Pharaoh Neco, set out to aid Assyria in its war with Babylon. Josiah tried to stop him. They met in battle at Megiddo. Josiah's army was defeated, and the king lost his life on the battlefield.

Josiah's defeat came only a few short years after his kingdom had begun to free itself from subjection to Assyria. It heralded the beginning of the end for Judah. For the next 23 years, until the kingdom eventually fell, it was no longer truly independent. Pharaoh Neco decided who would succeed Josiah as king. He chose Jehoiakim who he knew was pro-Egyptian.

Assyria's alliance with Egypt could not save its empire. In the year 605 B.C.E., the Assyrian army suffered a final defeat by the Babylonians in a battle at Carchemish, on the banks of the Euphrates River. Babylon now controlled all of the Fertile Crescent (including Judah), except for Egypt. However, the last three kings of Judah—Jehoiakim, his son Jehoiachin, and his uncle Zedekiah, son of Josiah—could not accept their subjection to Babylon. They hoped that with the help of Egypt they could regain their independence. In 598 B.C.E., Jehoiakim rebelled against Babylon in the false belief that Egypt would come to his aid. The uprising was quelled, Jehoiakim died on the battlefield, and Jehoiachin was exiled to Babylon together with more than 10,000 of the nation's upper class. Nebuchadnezzar, the king of Babylon, crowned Zedekiah, Jehoiachin's uncle, as king in Jerusalem.

Although Zedekiah was afraid to adopt an anti-Babylonian policy, he took the advice of his courtiers and in the ninth year of his reign he refused to pay tribute to Babylon. This was

30. Nebuchadnezzar II built this Road of Processions in the city of Babylon in the year 580 B.C.E.

tantamount to a declaration of war. Jerusalem was placed under a long and difficult siege, and in the year 586 B.C.E. the city surrendered. All of Jerusalem, including the Temple, was destroyed, and its people were sent into exile in Babylon along with all of the other citizens of Judah. The kingdom of Judah, established about 400 years earlier by David, had fallen.

The exile of the Judeans to Babylon was different from the exile of the Israelites to Assyria. First, the Babylonians did not scatter them, but settled them all in one place where the Jewish community could continue to exist. Secondly, these exiles were more united than the Israelites, and their cultural and religious traditions were stronger, particularly after Josiah's religious reforms. Their faith in the God of Israel was deeper than ever.

SARGON BOASTS OF THE CONQUEST OF SAMARIA

Several inscriptions were found carved in stone in Sargon's palace at Khorsabad near Nineveh, the capital of Assyria. In one of them, the king boasts of his conquest of Samaria. Scholars first succeeded in reading the inscription about 50 years ago.

This is what it says: "At the beginning of my royal rule I [besieged, conquered?]...the town of the Samarians....I led away as prisoners 27,290 inhabitants of it....The town I rebuilt better than it was before and settled therein people from countries which I myself had conquered. I placed an officer of mine as governor over them and imposed upon them tribute as for Assyrian citizens."

A small Jewish community was left in the Land of Israel. The Babylonian king appointed a Jewish governor over them—Gedaliah, son of Ahikam—but he was murdered and many people fled to Egypt.

5 · CULTURE AND RELIGION IN THE ISRAELITE KINGDOMS

1. Silver and bronze Canaanite idols found at the site of a temple in northern Eretz Yisrael. Most are female figures. The prophets fought against idol worship and other Canaanite influences on the Israelites.

2. A female face at a window was a popular decorative motif throughout the ancient East. This figure is made of ivory and was found in Mesopotamia. Similar pieces have been found in Eretz Yisrael. Some scholars believe it to be the depiction of a goddess in a pagan temple.

The period between the time of Solomon and the exile from Jerusalem in 586 B.C.E. is called the First Temple Period. This reflects the great importance the Temple in Jerusalem had in the nation's life.

The most important spiritual process taking place at that time was the molding of the religion of Israel—monotheism, or belief in one God. There were constant conflicts with the other religions held by the people of the ancient East. These were all polytheistic, which means that their religions were based on the belief in the existence of many gods. In the Book of Psalms—a collection of verse mostly from the First Temple Period—there is a passage which shows the huge difference between monotheism and all the other religions in the east. Here, the people are complaining that they feel alien amongst the other nations:

"Let the nations not say,
'Where now is their God?'
when our God is in heaven
and all that He wills He accomplishes.
Their idols are silver and gold,
the work of men's hands.
They have mouths, but cannot speak,
eyes, but cannot see;
they have ears, but cannot hear,
noses, but cannot smell;
they have hands, but cannot touch,
feet, but cannot walk;
they can make no sound in their throats." (Psalms 115:2-7).

The God of Israel, on the other hand, has no physical form.

Some of the Israelites found it difficult to cut themselves off completely from the influences of the other nations in Canaan and beyond with whom they came into contact, nations like Egypt, Edom, and Philistine. Such Israelites worshiped both idols and the God of Israel. At

1

2

44

certain times, idol worship grew so popular that it was considered an official religion in Jerusalem or Samaria. This happened during the time of King Ahab of Samaria, who married Jezebel, the daughter of the king of Tyre. During his reign the Canaanite religion, whose chief god was Baal, was given official status in Israel. In order to do this, the prophets clashed with the kings, their ministers, and the priests, and were ready to go against public opinion and even risk death.

The greatest number of the early prophets lived mainly up until the middle of the 9th century B.C.E. They lived in communities with their

Israel. The same thing happened in Jerusalem, the capital of the Kingdom of Judah, especially during the reign of King Manasseh, when Assyrian control of the Land of Israel was strongest. Manasseh made the Assyrian rites part of the official ritual in the Temple.

THE PROPHETS FIGHT BACK

The prophets, spiritual leaders who saw themselves as the emissaries of the God of Israel, devoted their lives to a single goal: shaping the spiritual and community life of the Israeli nation according to the moral and religious principles of the God of

disciples, who were known as the "sons of the prophets." Their primary concern was to live according to faith in the God of Israel. Some of the prophets were welcomed into the royal courts. Gad and Nathan prophesied in the courts of David and Solomon; Micahiah and Elijah were advisors to Ahab; and it is said of Elisha that he prophesied for King Jehoram of Samaria. It was especially in times of war that the kings consulted these prophets, in order to learn of their chances for victory.

However, there were also many conflicts between the prophets and the kings. Nathan reprimanded David

3. Stone altars on which animals were sacrificed have been found both inside and outside temples. These are from an Israelite temple built in the 9th century B.C.E. at Arad, on the edge of the Judean Desert.

4. Many artists have envisioned the prophets, who preached the precepts of religion and morality, as wrathful figures. This woodcut of a prophet was done by the modern German painter, Emil Nolde.

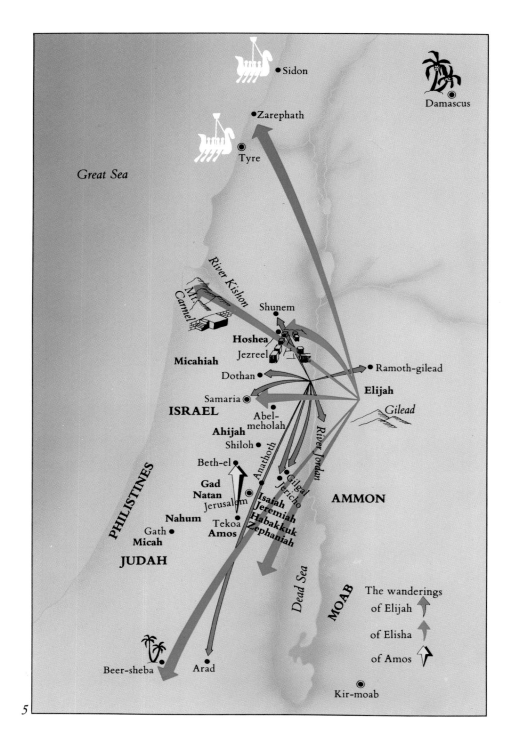

5

In the middle of the 9th century B.C.E., a different sort of prophet appeared on the scene who did not live in groups with their disciples, but as individuals. The first of these prophets was Amos. Isaiah and Jeremiah were prophets of the same type. Most of them were not connected with the royal courts and their prophecies did not concern the kings' chances of success in battle. Also unlike the earlier prophets, they did not perform many miracles. The two outstanding features of these prophets were: 1: their belief that in the eyes of the God of Israel, moral principles came before anything else, even before the observance of ritual laws; and 2: their words were written down, usually in very beautiful verse considered even today some of the world's greatest literature. These prophecies were written either by the prophets themselves or by their disciples who recorded what they said.

The prophets shaped the spiritual life of the Israeli nation not only in the First Temple Period, but for the future as well. The ideas of Jesus and his disciples were also based on the words of the prophets. From the few short quotations below, we can learn of the main ideas they affirmed.

1. The prophets fought against the oppression of the weak by the rulers and wealthy people.

5. The prophets and the sites where they were active.

6. Mount Carmel, where Elijah triumphed over the prophets of the god Baal. This traditional site is known as Muhraka, "the fire," and houses a monastery, and a statue of the prophet.

7. (On page 47) "You will drink from the wadi, and I have commanded the ravens to feed you there", (I Kings 17:4) said the Lord to Elijah. The painting is from a 14th century Russian book.

harshly for his violations of the Ten Commandments about murder, adultery, and coveting. Ahijah of Shiloh rebuked Jeroboam and declared that his son would die and his dynasty be overthrown as punishment for his having worshiped foreign gods. Elijah constantly fought with Ahab because the king allowed the Canaanite worship of Baal into his kingdom. These prophets never recorded their words. All we know of what they did and said comes from the stories and legends in the Books of Samuel and Kings.

6

"Thus said the LORD: For three transgressions of Israel,
For four, I will not revoke it:
Because they have sold for silver
Those whose cause was just,
And the needy for a pair of sandals.
You who trample the heads of the poor into the dust of the ground, and make the humble walk a twisted course!" (Amos 2:6-7);

7

"Hear this word, you...
On the hill of Samaria—
Who defraud the poor,
Who rob the needy....
My Lord God swears by His holiness:
Behold, days are coming upon you
When you will be carried off in
    baskets....
And flung on the refuse heap."
(Amos 4:1-3);

"Alas, she has become a harlot,
The faithful city
That was filled with justice,
Where righteousness dwelt—
But now murderers.
Your silver has turned to dross;
Your wine is cut with water.

AHAB AND ELIJAH

The relationship between King Ahab and the Prophet Elijah is particularly interesting. It teaches us of the constant conflicts between those who were faithful to the God of Israel, led by the prophets, and the worshipers of idols and the Canaanite god, Baal. It was Jezebel, the wife of Ahab, who promoted the worship of Baal in Israel.

Baal was the god of fertility who brought the rains. Without rain, there could be no agriculture in Israel since it had so few rivers. The Bible relates that after a long period of drought, Jezebel ordered all the prophets of the God of Israel to be put to death. She probably hoped that this would appease Baal and he would bring them rain and save the land from a severe famine. The prophets of Israel had to hide from Jezebel and Elijah fled to the desert.

After three years of famine in Israel, Elijah appeared before Ahab and proposed a public test between himself and the prophets of Baal to see which of them could cause the rain to fall. The people gathered on Mount Carmel at the altar of Baal, near the altar of the God of Israel which had been destroyed by order of Jezebel.

Elijah said to the people: "'How long will you keep hopping between two opinions? If the Lord is God, follow Him; and if Baal, follow him!... I am the only prophet of the Lord left, while the prophets of Baal are four hundred and fifty men. Let two young bulls be given to us. Let them choose one bull, cut it up, and lay it on the wood, but let them not apply fire; I will prepare the other bull, and lay it on the wood, and will not apply fire. You will then invoke your god by name, and I will invoke the Lord by name; and let us agree: the god who responds with fire, that one is God.' And all the people answered, 'Very good!'" (I Kings 18:21-24).

So the prophets of Baal prayed to their gods all day—but nothing happened. Now it was Elijah's turn. He prepared the bull for sacrifice, and then uttered a short prayer: "Answer me, O Lord, answer me, that this people may know that You, O Lord, are God; for You have turned their hearts backward." (I Kings 18:37).

Suddenly the wood on the altar caught fire. Elijah had won. He called on the people to seize the prophets of Baal and kill them. Elijah then turned to Ahab and informed him that it would rain, and this too happened as he said, and a heavy rain began to fall. The land was saved from famine. The God of Israel had triumphed over Baal, the god of Jezebel and of Tyre, the city from which she came.

Another event that shows the difference between the religion of Tyre and that of Israel is related in I Kings, chapter 21.

Naboth the Jezreelite had a vineyard near Ahab's palace. The king wanted it, but Naboth refused to sell his inheritance. The king was furious. On returning to the palace, he met his wife. Jezebel had grown up in a culture that allowed the king to do as he pleased. She laughed at Ahab and bribed witnesses to testify falsely that Naboth had blasphemed God and the king. Naboth was found guilty and put to death. His land became the property of the king.

Elijah did not remain silent in the face of this abuse of the king's power. He appeared before Ahab and stated fearlessly: "Thus said the Lord: Would you murder and take possession?... In the very place where the dogs lapped up Naboth's blood, the dogs will lap up your blood too." (I Kings 21:19).

The fact that Ahab did not punish Elijah for speaking to him in this way, shows us how highly Elijah was regarded. Even Jezebel could not talk her husband into harming Elijah.

Your rulers are rogues
And cronies of thieves,
Every one avid for presents
And greedy for gifts;
They do not judge the case of the
  orphan,
And the widow's cause never reaches
  them." (Isaiah 1:21-23).

2. The prophets fought against idol worship and considered it the main reason for the immorality of the people. They believed the tragedies that befell the nation were punishment for their lack of faith in the God of Israel and lack of obedience to His Law.

Like dew so early gone;
Like chaff whirled away from the
  threshing floor.
And like smoke from a lattice."
(Hosea 13:1-3).

3. The prophets did not only criticize Israel, but also prophesied against the pride and evil of other nations—Aram, Assyria, Babylon, Egypt, and others. Isaiah, for example, spoke out against the king of Babylon who believed that he, and not God, determined the fate of the world.

"How are you fallen from heaven,
O Shining One, son of Dawn!
How are you felled to earth,
O vanquisher of nations!
Once you thought in your heart,
'I will climb to the sky;
Higher than the stars of God
I will set my throne.
I will sit in the mount of assembly,
On the summit of Zaphon:
I will mount the back of a cloud—
I will match the Most High.'"
(Isaiah 14:12-14).

8. This illustration from a 15th century Jewish prayer book (the Rothschild siddur), shows Moses receiving the Tablets of the Law on Mount Sinai. According to Biblical tradition, it was here that the Israelites committed themselves to a belief in one God.

9. The High Priest in his ceremonial robes and the ritual vessels used for sacrifices appear in this 15th century painting.

10. (On page 49) According to Jewish tradition, the leviathan—shown in this illustration from a 13th century French manuscript—is one of the animals whose meat will be eaten by the righteous at the time of redemption in the Last Days.

"Assuredly, thus said the Lord: I am going to bring upon them disaster from which they will not be able to escape. Then they will cry out to me, but I will not listen to them. And the townsmen of Judah and the inhabitants of Jerusalem will go and cry out to the gods to which they sacrifice; but they will not be able to rescue them in their time of disaster." (Jeremiah 11:11-12);
"When Ephraim spoke piety,
He was exalted in Israel;
But he incurred guilt through Baal,
And so he died.
And now they go on sinning;
They have made them molten images,
Idols, by their skill, from their silver,
Wholly the work of craftsmen.
Yet for these they appoint men to
  sacrifice;
They are wont to kiss calves!
Assuredly,
They shall be like morning clouds,

4. In addition to their criticism of what was happening at the time, the prophets also drew a picture of the world in the future, at the end of

time—the Last Days. In this way they defined the goals to which men should aspire. The leaders of the modern world had good reason for carving these words of Isaiah at the entrance to the United Nations building in New York City:

"And it shall come to pass in the last days, that the mountain of the Lord's

10

11

house shall be established in the top of the mountains, and shall be exalted above the hills; and all nations shall flow unto it. And many people shall go and say, Come ye, and let us go up to the mountain of the Lord, to the

THE PROPHET JEREMIAH

The story of Jeremiah is one of the most moving stories in the Bible. We know much more about this prophet than we do of any of the others.

Jeremiah was born in the second half of the 7th century B.C.E. in a small village near Jerusalem called Anathoth. According to his own account, he first heard the voice of God calling upon him to prophesy to the nations when he was a young boy. He tried to evade this mission, saying that he was still too young. But he could not free himself from the divine commandment. He accepted the responsibility of carrying the word of God to the nations and to the kingdoms "to uproot and to pull down, to destroy and to overthrow, to build and to plant" (Jeremiah 1:10).

Throughout his life, Jeremiah suffered from an internal conflict between his lack of desire to be a prophet and his feeling that he must obey the word of God. During one of the many crises he underwent in his life, he bitterly expressed his feelings about his sacred mission:
"You enticed me, O Lord, and I was enticed;
You overpowered me and You prevailed.
I have become a constant laughingstock,
Everyone jeers at me.
For every time I speak, I must cry out,
Must shout, 'Lawlessness and rapine!'
For the word of the Lord causes me
Constant disgrace and contempt.
I thought, 'I will not mention Him,
No more will I speak in His name'—
But [His word] was like a raging fire in my heart,
Shut up in my bones;
I could not hold it in, I was helpless." (Jeremiah 20:7-9).

All his life, Jeremiah clashed with the ministers, kings, and priests. He was imprisoned at least three times and his life was often in danger. And it was all because he could not stop preaching to the nation and its leaders. He also had to fight the "false prophets"—people who preached just the opposite of what he said and claimed that they, and not Jeremiah, spoke the word of God.

Jeremiah delivered his prophecies in the streets of Jerusalem, at the gates of the Temple, and in the royal court. He also wrote down many of his prophecies and read them out to the people and the king. In this way he proved that he had warned of a threat to Israel from a northern kingdom many years before Babylon defeated Assyria.

Most of Jeremiah's prophecies are harsh criticisms of two things: 1: the ingratitude of the nation toward its God, shown by their worship of idols along with their worship of the God of Israel; and 2: the refusal of the kings of Judah to accept the judgment of God and subject themselves peacefully to the king of Babylon. Jeremiah warned the kings that if they rebelled against Babylon it would cause the destruction of Jerusalem. Until the very last days of the final siege of the city in the year 586 B.C.E., he tried unsuccessfully to convince King Zedekiah to surrender to Babylon and save the city.

When Jerusalem fell to the Babylonians, Jeremiah remained in the land of Judah. Later, with the rest of the people left in Judah, he went to Egypt, and there he died.

12

11. (On page 49) Jerusalem and its Temple—seen in this illustration from the Hamburg Haggadah produced in Germany in the 18th century—have a special place in Jewish tradition: in the Last Days the city will be rebuilt and stand forever as a spiritual center for the entire world.

12. In Ezekiel's vision of the "dry bones," the prophet describes how the dead will be brought back to life in the Last Days. This depiction of his vision is part of a fresco found in a 3rd century synagogue at Dura Europos in northern Mesopotamia.

house of the God of Jacob; and he will teach us of his ways, and we will walk in his paths: for out of Zion shall go forth the law, and the word of the Lord from Jerusalem. And he shall judge among the nations, and shall decide among many people: and they shall beat their swords into plowshares, and their spears into pruning hooks: nation shall not lift up sword against nation, neither shall they learn war any more."
(Isaiah 2:2-4).

Other forms of writing were also produced during the First Temple Period. Some were poetic works which described the thoughts and questions of a man of faith. These were collected in the Book of Psalms.

Stories of Israel's past—its ancestors, heroes, and history—were also written at this time. They are the basis of our knowledge of the early periods in the history of the Israelite nation. A great many proverbs were also composed. These sought to explain the laws governing the world of human beings and nature. And, of course, there was much legal literature concerning both society and religion.

All of these writings were collected in the Bible. They were the spiritual armor that the people of Israel took with them into exile. This extensive and unique cultural heritage made it possible for the people to survive as a nation in exile, and eventually to return to their homeland.

CULTURE AND RELIGION IN THE
ISRAELITE KINGDOMS

6 · EXILE TO BABYLON AND RETURN TO ZION

After Jerusalem was destroyed, not many of the people from the kingdom of Judah remained in the Land of Israel. Those who stayed were either working people who had not been sent into exile, or Samaritans, who had evolved into a separate nation since the destruction of Samaria in 721 B.C.E.. With the elite of the nation exiled to Babylon, the cultural center of the Israelites now moved there, although there was also a community of exiles in Egypt. Since the surviving Israelites were originally from Judah, from this time on they are also called "Jews."

In Babylon, the priests continued to preserve and develop the religious culture. There were even two prophets in Babylon—Ezekiel and an anonymous prophet known as Deutero-Isaiah (the second Isaiah) because his words of comfort are included in the Book of Isaiah (chapters 40-55). He prophesied that the nation would soon return to its land and rebuild the Temple.

Changes were now taking place in the region. Persia had taken over most of the area from Babylon.

KING CYRUS OF PERSIA

When Cyrus became king of Persia, his country was still a small subject land. Cyrus conquered his neighboring land, Media, and became the king of Persia and Media. He then went on to conquer lands in Asia Minor. After he defeated Croesus, king of Lydia, he rebelled openly against Babylon. Cyrus took advantage of the fact that the priests of the city of Babylon were angered by their king, Nabonidus. The king had raised Sin, the moon god, to a higher status than their chief god, Marduk. Cyrus declared that he

1. The tomb of King Cyrus of Persia at Pasargadae in the central Iranian plateau.

2. A soldier of the Persian royal guard, holding a spear and carrying a bow and arrows on his back. The outer wall of the royal palace at Susa—one of the two Persian capitals—was adorned with glazed bricks bearing the figures of soldiers.

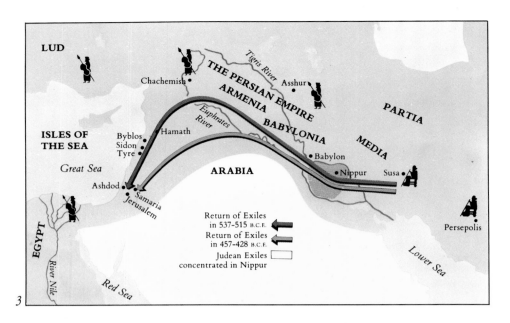

In 539 B.C.E., Cyrus issued an edict to the Jewish exiles in Babylon. One of the versions of this edict appears in the last verse of the Bible. It reads: "Thus said King Cyrus of Persia: The LORD God of Heaven has given me all the kingdoms of the earth, and has charged me with building Him a House in Jerusalem, which is in Judah. Anyone of you of all His people, the Lord His God be with him and let him go up." (II Chronicles 36:23).

FROM BABYLON TO JERUSALEM

This declaration was the start of a

3. The return of the exiles from Babylon to Judah.

4. This section of a fresco from the palace of Darius I, the grandson of Cyrus, at Persepolis—one of the two capitals of the Persian Empire—shows two soldiers and their weapons. Their helmets indicate the countries they come from.

5. One of the walls of the palace of Darius I at Persepolis decorated with frescos showing the king on his throne and below a procession of people bearing tribute.

was sent by Marduk to rescue Babylon from Nabonidus. When Cyrus defeated Babylon in 540 B.C.E., Persia became the strongest power in the whole of the ancient East.

Cyrus adopted an entirely new policy toward the conquered nations. Instead of abolishing the local religions, he claimed to be the emissary of each local god. He was therefore very popular among the people who were previously subject to Babylon. Cyrus wanted the exiles of Judah to return to Jerusalem. There they could again live as a nation, while remaining loyal to the Persian Empire.

period known as the Return to Zion. Many people considered this the fulfillment of redemption promised by the prophets. They organized themselves to return to Jerusalem, led by the high priest Joshua, son of Jehozadak, and Zerubbabel, son of Shealtiel, a member of the royal family.

When the exiles reached Jerusalem, they found the city in ruins. They began to rebuild it. Their main purpose in returning to their homeland was to reestablish the Temple, but because of their serious economic problems this had to be put off for a while. The Second Temple in

EXILE TO BABYLON AND
RETURN TO ZION

Jerusalem was finally dedicated in 516 B.C.E., more than 20 years after the start of the Return to Zion. It was much smaller and simpler than the First Temple. Nevertheless, it was of great importance. With the Temple again standing in Jerusalem, the city's rebirth as the major cultural and spiritual center of the Jewish people was assured. The author of the Book of Ezra describes the people's reaction to the dedication ceremony: "Many of the priests and Levites and the chiefs of the clans, the old men who had seen the first house, wept loudly at the sight of the founding of this house.

Many others shouted joyously at the top of their voices. The people could not distinguish the shouts of joy from the people's weeping, for the people raised a great shout, the sound of which could be heard from afar." (Ezra 3:12-13).

At the beginning of the Second Temple Period, the Jewish population of Jerusalem was very small. Most of the people, and particularly the richer ones, preferred to live in comfort in Babylon than to move to a country in ruins and to a city surrounded by enemies. A severe drought in the Land of Israel at that time made life even

6

7

6. *A typical landscape of Judah, home of the returning exiles.*

7. *The leg of a pehah's throne, found in Eretz Yisrael. The pehah was the governor of the district, appointed by the Persian king. Nehemiah, one of the leaders of the returning exiles, was pehah of Judah.*

8. *To this day the Samaritans preserve their ancient customs, such as the Passover sacrifice on Mount Gerizim shown here.*

8

harder. The Jewish community in Jerusalem was sadly troubled. Was this the redemption promised by Isaiah, Jeremiah, Ezekiel, and the other prophets? Was this the divine mercy they had looked forward to?

Things began to improve around the middle of the 5th century B.C.E. Two new leaders—Ezra and Nehemiah—arrived in Jerusalem at the head of another group of exiles from Babylon. Ezra was a scribe, a learned person who not only copied sacred texts in Babylon, but also edited and interpreted them. When he arrived in the Land of Israel, he brought the Law of Moses to the entire nation. This was of major importance in shaping the national and religious life of the Jewish people for all future generations. Jewish tradition compares Ezra to Moses, stating that "Ezra would have been worthy of giving the Law to Israel if Moses had not come before him."

Ezra's contribution was largely religious and cultural, while

Nehemiah was a political and social leader. He was a high minister in the court of Darius, the king of Persia. When he heard of the harsh conditions in Jerusalem, he asked Darius to appoint him *pehah*—the king's governor—in Jerusalem. Darius agreed. As soon as Nehemiah arrived in Jerusalem, he realized that the first thing they needed was a wall to protect the city. With a wall around it, traveling traders could take refuge in Jerusalem and be safe. Thus Jerusalem would acquire the status of a real capital. A wall was raised around Jerusalem (in about 445 B.C.E.), despite the objections of the neighboring nations—the Ammonites, Moabites, Arabs, and Samaritans— who felt threatened by the independence of the Jewish people. Because of the difficult economic circumstances, Nehemiah did not collect the taxes he was entitled to. He even demanded that land be returned to the poor farmers who had been forced to sell their property.

The combined efforts of Ezra and Nehemiah renewed the strength of Jerusalem. By the beginning of the 4th century B.C.E., Jerusalem was regaining its status as the spiritual and political center of the Jewish people.

At this time, the gap between the Jews and the Samaritans grew even wider. The Samaritans had lived in Samaria continuously since the exile of Israel in 721 B.C.E. They felt they had greater rights in the land than the Jews who only recently had returned from Babylon. The Samaritans had also developed their own culture. Although it was based on the Law of Moses, they did not accept Ezra's interpretations of it. For this reason, the Samaritans were not allowed to take part in the rebuilding of the Temple, and they did not permit their children to be educated with the Jews. From this time on, the Jews and the Samaritans were two separate and hostile nations.

9. "By the rivers of Babylon, there we sat, sat and wept, as we thought of Zion" (Psalms 137:1), in a painting by the 19th century French artist Delacroix. Throughout their exile, the Jews continued to lament the destruction of Jerusalem and dreamed of the day they would return.

10. The district of Judah to which the exiles returned.

9

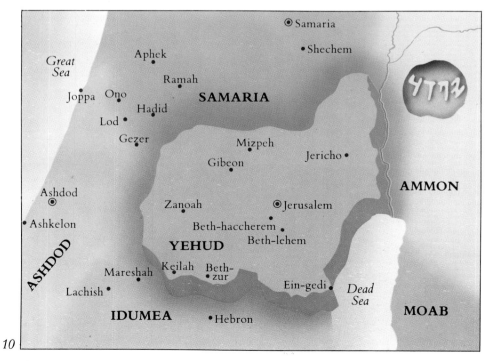

10

WHY JERUSALEM?

After almost 70 years in Babylon, the returning exiles from the Kingdom of Judah resettled in Jerusalem, which was then in ruins. Why? What tied them to this city? The answer can be found in the history of this very special place.

Jerusalem was founded around 5,000 years ago by the Jebusites, a Canaanite tribe. The city was erected on a hill protected on three sides by deep canyons, and covered an area no larger than eight acres. It was therefore relatively easy to fortify the city and defend it from attack. Only a few clay utensils have been discovered from this early period, but archeologists have found burial caves, an Egyptian seal, and even a tunnel supplying water to the city from a slightly later time.

After the Israelite settlement, Canaanites continued to live in Jerusalem, until it was conquered around the year 1000 B.C.E. by King David, who made it the capital of his kingdom, uniting North and South. It was also known as the City of David. David's son, Solomon, was the first of the great builders of Jerusalem. He erected a magnificent Temple on a site believed to be chosen by God, and built his palace adjoining the Temple so as to unify political and religious leadership in one place. It remained the capital of all the kings of the House of David until its destruction four centuries later.

Many people coveted the land and its capital. As early as the reign of Rehoboam, the son of Solomon (925 B.C.E.), it was invaded by Shishak, the king of Egypt. This time Jerusalem was saved by its wealth. Shishak agreed not to destroy the city in exchange for the treasures of the royal house and the Temple treasury.

The kings of Judah continued to enlarge the city. The most ambitious of them was Uzziah. During his reign, Jerusalem grew so

1.

2

3

1. The Western Wall of the Temple Mount, also known as the Wailing Wall, has survived since the time of the Second Temple and the conquest of Jerusalem by the Romans. Since that time, Jews have come here to mourn the destruction of the Temple and to pray for redemption.

2. A view of Jerusalem today. In the center, the Temple Mount surrounded by its wall and the two mosques erected on it—the Dome of the Rock on the right and El Aksa on the left.

3. Since the early days of Christianity, Jerusalem has attracted Christian pilgrims and many churches have been built in the city. The bell towers of some of these churches, along with the domes of several mosques, can be seen in this painting by the English artist Turner from the 19th century.

large that the city walls and fortifications had to be extended. During the time of Hezekiah, who reigned in the late 8th century B.C.E., Jerusalem repelled an Assyrian attack. This strengthened the popular belief that God would never allow His city to fall to its enemies. Nevertheless, more than a century later, Jerusalem could not withstand the attack by Nebuchadnezzar, king of Babylon. In the year 586 B.C.E., he conquered the city, destroying the Temple, and sent its inhabitants into exile.

Throughout the long years of exile in Babylon, the exiles did not lose their faith that Jerusalem would be rebuilt. The prophets all promised that within seventy years the people would return to the City of David. Indeed, this prophecy came true when Cyrus of Persia issued his famous edict.

By the time the exiles returned, Jerusalem had become a small, unfortified city threatened on all its borders by neighboring powers. It was only when the Second Temple was erected in 516 B.C.E., and the city wall rebuilt, that Jerusalem began to regain its former status. Slowly it grew stronger and

4. Jerusalem at the time of Kings David and Solomon, 9th-8th centuries B.C.E.

5. Jerusalem at the time of Nehemiah, c. 440 B.C.E.

6. Jerusalem at the time of the Hasmoneans, 140-160 B.C.E.

7. Jerusalem at the time of Herod, 30-4 B.C.E.

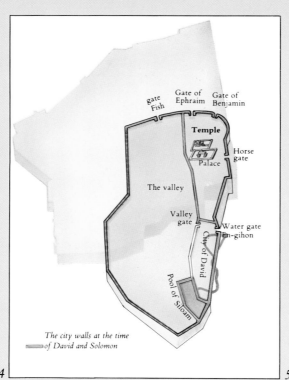

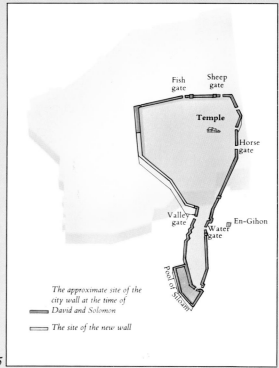

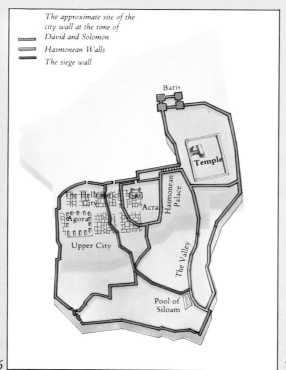

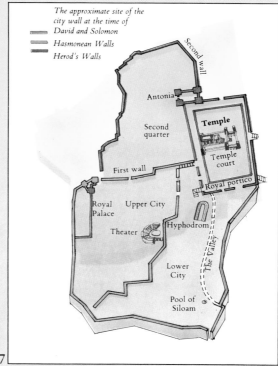

The area of the Old City today

The area of the city in the period represented on the map

Water channels and pools

larger, until it again became the most important city in Eretz Yisrael. During the Hellenistic period (described in chapters 7 and 8), it was the cultural center of the entire region. In the second century B.C.E., when the Jews won their independence from Greece, the kingdom was reestablished in Jerusalem under the Hasmoneans.

The next great builder of Jerusalem was Herod, who ruled at the end of the first century B.C.E. He strengthened the city's fortifications and renovated the Temple, making it even more magnificent than the

8

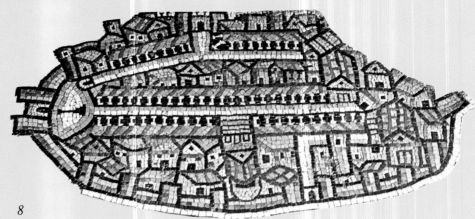

9

10

earlier one. Even the Jewish sages, who despised Herod, could not deny the Temple's extraordinary beauty.

During this period, Jews from neighboring countries came to Jerusalem for the pilgrimage festivals. The city's streets were widened and trade flourished. It is not surprising that it was here that Jesus of Nazareth chose to preach his ideas. Here, too, he died at the hands of the Romans. To this day, millions of Christian pilgrims visit the Church of the Holy Sepulcher, built on the site where Jesus is traditionally believed to have been buried. After the death of Jesus, his followers gathered in Jerusalem and established the first Christian community in the city.

When Jerusalem was destroyed by the Romans in the year 70 C.E., it ceased to be the center of Jewish life. However, both Jews and Christians persevered in their faith in it as a holy city, and continued to make their pilgrimages there. Later, in the 7th century C.E., when Islam was born Jerusalem then became a holy city for Moslems as well. According to their belief, it was in Jerusalem, on the site of the ruined Temple, that their prophet, Muhammad, saw Abraham, Moses, and Jesus and ascended to heaven.

Today, Jerusalem is the capital of the modern State of Israel. In the Old City, the Jewish, Moslem, and Christian quarters have been preserved, along with ancient synagogues, churches, and mosques. They bear witness to the holy status of Jerusalem for three of the world's great monotheistic religions.

8. Jerusalem in the mosaic floor of a 6th century church in Madeba, Jordan. Note the broad street in the center built by the Romans and known as the Cardo.

9. David's Tower in the Old City Wall was built on the foundations of the wall Herod erected. It is the traditional site of the Tomb of King David.

10. A reconstruction of Jerusalem in the period of the Second Temple. In the center, the Temple and Temple Mount; on the right, Fortress Antonia, built by Herod and named for Mark Antony.

7 · GREEK RULE AND THE HASMONEAN KINGS

After Greece defeated Persia, the Greek emperor, Alexander the Great, gained control of more and more territory until he had formed a larger empire than ever before known in the East.

The Greek conquerors believed that the Hellenic (from *Hellas*, the ancient name for Greece) civilization was superior to all others. In a certain sense, they may have been right, if we consider how highly developed was the Greek social order (democracy), poetry (Homer), philosophy (Socrates, Plato, and Aristotle), mathematics (Pythagoras), sculpture, and architecture. The Greeks encouraged the spread of their culture to all the lands they conquered. Both people and nations were judged by whether or not they adopted the Greek culture (were Hellenized), rather than whether or not they were actually Greek.

The Greeks themselves came from a large number of different tribes. Even Alexander was not from Athens, the center of Greek civilization, but from Macedonia. The soldiers in his huge army belonged to dozens of different nations and tribes. When Alexander died (in 323 B.C.E.), his mighty empire

was divided up among his heirs. Each of them stationed soldiers in his own territory, and the soldiers set up city-states (*poleis*) of the sort that existed in Greece itself. Thus even after the great empire was broken up, Hellenic culture was preserved in these city-states which were established throughout the East. This whole period is therefore known as the Hellenistic Period.

Our knowledge of the period comes mainly from books written by historians of that time, from literature of the period, and from archeological finds which help us to understand and visualize the historical facts.

ERETZ YISRAEL AFTER THE GREEK CONQUEST

When Alexander's empire was divided up, Eretz Yisrael found itself in the middle between two rival Hellenistic kingdoms: the Seleucid kingdom whose center was in Syria, and the Ptolemaic kingdom centered in Egypt.

Immediately after Alexander's death, war broke out between these two kingdoms, and Eretz Yisrael changed hands several times. Finally, Ptolemy I, king of Egypt, conquered the land, which was then ruled by the Ptolemies between 301 and 200 B.C.E.

The Seleucids never reconciled themselves to this situation, and periodically tried to reconquer the region. In the year 200 B.C.E., Antiochus III, king of Syria, defeated the Egyptian king in a battle fought near the sources of the River Jordan. Eretz Yisrael was now under Seleucid rule.

During this time, Judah, now known as Judea, was developing from a small and impoverished Persian province into a densely populated and prosperous land in its own right. As agriculture improved, local and international trade developed, and Jerusalem, the capital, became one of the richest cities in the entire region. The small Jewish population at the start of the Return to Zion grew so large that there was not enough room for them to live in and around Jerusalem. Many Jews began to settle elsewhere throughout Eretz Yisrael. Major Jewish centers were established in Samaria, the Galilee, and on the eastern side of the Jordan.

Although many non-Jews also lived there, Eretz Yisrael again became a largely Jewish land. And even though a large part of the nation lived outside the borders of Judea, there was still the feeling that the Jews had returned to settle in their homeland.

Judea was now autonomous, which means that the Jewish people governed

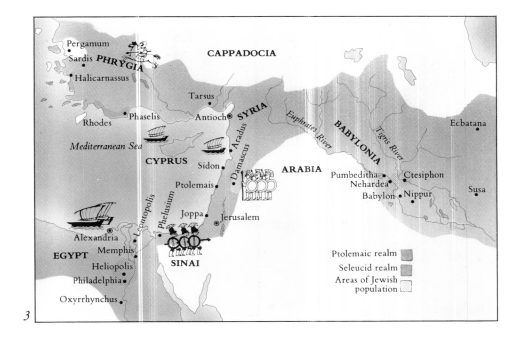

3

3. Alexander's empire was divided up between the Ptolemies (in the south) and the Seleucids (in the north).

4. This illustration from a 16th century Persian manuscript depicts the battle between Darius III and Alexander the Great.

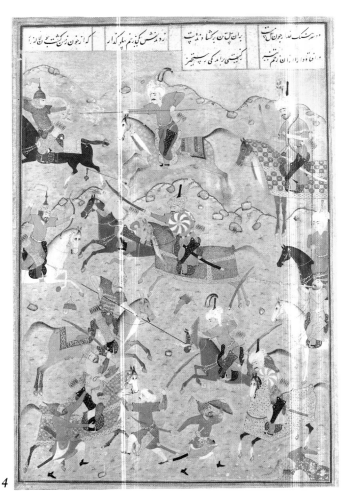

4

5

6

7

5. The phalanx depicted here was one of the strategies Alexander used against his enemies. The soldiers marched in tight formations, with those in front attacking with their long spears and those behind holding them above their heads to protect against the weapons hurled at them.

6. A gold coin from the 2nd century B.C.E. bearing the name of Arsinoe, a Ptolemaic princess. The horns of plenty are filled with fruit, the gift of the Nile.

7. The eagle was the symbol of the Ptolemaic kingdom. It appears here on a coin of Ptolemy I from the year 300 B.C.E.

8. A colony of former Macedonian soldiers was established at Samaria. Excavations have uncovered this round tower, part of the town's fortifications from the Hellenistic period.

8

themselves in all internal matters: legislation, education, and religion. The Temple in Jerusalem which was the cultural and religious center of the Jews was recognized even by the Greek conquerors. The High Priest of the Temple was not only the religious leader, but the political leader as well. Together with a Council of Elders, he was the head of the Jewish community and represented it before the authorities.

These leaders also levied taxes on the Jewish population. Tax collectors from rich families were appointed for this purpose, and they received a certain percentage of what they collected in payment. Under such a system, it is not surprising that they sometimes demanded more from the people than was actually due.

There was also a sector of the Jewish population in Jerusalem that had greater contact with the Greek authorities. These people were more influenced by Hellenistic culture than the rest of the populace. They were known as "Hellenists," a term which was considered to be something of an insult by the rest of the Jewish population.

The Edicts of Antiochus and the Hasmonean Revolt

There was a change for the worse in the relations between the Hellenistic rulers and the Jewish population during the reign of Antiochus IV (Epiphanes), who ruled from 175 to 164 B.C.E. The Romans were becoming a major power in the East. They defeated Antiochus III in battle, and he had to relinquish control of Asia Minor, an important part of his empire. The Seleucid kingdom was

Yisrael was increasing.

In 168 B.C.E., Antiochus defeated Ptolemy. However, the Romans had just conquered the Macedonian kingdom in northeast Syria and were now a direct threat to the Seleucid kingdom. When they demanded that Antiochus retreat from Egypt, he had no choice but to obey. This sign of Antiochus's weakness raised the hope in Jerusalem that the Jews could free themselves from his rule. A revolt broke out in the city, but it was quickly put down. In order to make

9

9. This fresco was found in a tomb from the early Hellenistic period (3rd century B.C.E.) at Mareshah to the east of the River Jordan. Paintings very similar in style have been found in Greek temples.

10. A Hanukkah lamp of silver and gilt from 19th century Poland. The festival of Hanukkah commemorates the victory of the Hasmoneans over the Seleucids and the regaining of Jewish independence. It is one of the happiest holidays in the Jewish calendar.

threatened in the north by the Parthians, and in the south by the Ptolemies. This situation put a heavy financial burden on the Seleucids, and so they raised the taxes in Judea. Moreover, in order to unify his kingdom, Antiochus IV ordered that all of the inhabitants, by force of law, adopt Hellenistic culture. As part of this policy, he even meddled in the affairs of the Temple in Jerusalem, and arranged the election of a high priest who would support him. Judea lost its autonomy, and hostility between the Greek authorities and most of the Jewish population of Eretz

10

sure that such a thing did not happen again, Antiochus settled a large number of non-Jews in Jerusalem. They and the Hellenists—the Jews who adopted Greek culture—were put in charge of governing the city.

The following year, Antiochus IV issued edicts which enraged the Jewish population even more. He forbade them to observe the commandments of their religion, ordered them to bow down to idols and to eat forbidden foods; he even turned the Temple into a shrine to the Greek god Zeus. This was the first time in their history that the Jews had been subjected to edicts of this sort. Throughout the land, the people rebelled. The Seleucids were driven out and for the first time since the destruction of the First Temple, an independent Jewish kingdom was established in Jerusalem—the Hasmonean kingdom.

Mattathias played a role in the outbreak of the revolt. He was a priest from the village of Modi'in who served in the Temple in Jerusalem, but returned to his village following the edicts of Antiochus. He was persecuted by the Greek authorities for preaching against the Hellenists and had to flee with his family from Modi'in. They hid in the Judean Desert, and there Mattathias began to organize an uprising against the Greeks. He was joined by people from Jewish villages in the mountains around Jerusalem. When Mattathias died, his son Judah became the leader of the revolt. One after the other,

11

11. This silver coin commemorates Alexander the Great's victory over the Indians in Punjab. Alexander is seen on horseback attacking the Indian king who is riding an elephant. Elephants were used in battle because their huge size frightened horses and their great weight could crush foot soldiers. Some were even trained to catch enemy soldiers in their trunks and impale them on their tusks.

12. The leaders of the revolt against the Seleucids were known as the Maccabees. Here the rebellion is shown in an illustration from a 13th century French manuscript. At the upper left, Greek soldiers burst into the Temple. At the upper right, Jews are forced to bow down before the idol of Zeus. The lower half shows the battle, with the Greeks on the right, identifiable by their shields. Note that the armor and weapons are typical of those used by the knights and Crusaders of the Middle Ages, the time when this illustration was drawn.

12

situation and succeeded in leading his army back to Jerusalem. In 152 B.C.E., he was elected to the post of high priest. From then on, Jerusalem remained independent, although officially it remained part of the Seleucid kingdom. There were two contenders to the Seleucid throne, and since Jonathan had a large army, each

13. Tunnels were dug beneath the Temple Mount so that people could hide in them or move secretly from place to place.

14. This etching from a German manuscript depicts the Hasmonean revolt. Lysias used dozens of elephants in the battle at Bet Zacharia. One of them crushed Mattathias's son Eleazar to death.

15. In this region in the Judean Hills the Hasmoneans hid and planned their revolt.

Judah defeated the generals of the Greek army.

Judah conquered Jerusalem (164 B.C.E.), purified the Temple, and enabled the priests to resume their authority over the ritual. These events are commemorated in the festival of Hanukkah (from the Hebrew word for "dedication"), celebrated by Jews every winter to this day. For eight days, candles are lit in memory of the rededication of the Temple.

Even after Jerusalem was taken, Judea remained officially subject to the Seleucid kingdom in Syria. The Seleucid army attempted repeatedly to reconquer the city. Control of Jerusalem changed hands several times, until the year 160 B.C.E. when Judah was killed in a battle with the Seleucid general, Bacchides.

The major battles were now waged between the two Jewish camps: the Hellenists who advocated Greek culture and were content with Seleucid rule, and those who wanted independence, led by Judah's brothers, Jonathan, Simeon, and Johanan.

The Seleucid court was also the scene of internal rivalries at this time. Jonathan took advantage of the

Hannah and her Seven Sons

The edicts of Antiochus are remembered not only by historians, but also in folk legends. One of the most famous stories about the period is told in the Second Book of Maccabees. It concerns a mother of amazing courage and faith who saw all seven of her sons put to death on the same day.

Hannah was a deeply religious woman who raised her seven sons to love and worship God. One day they were caught observing Jewish law in defiance of Antiochus's edicts. Antiochus ordered them all to be put to death. As the turn came for each to die, Hannah comforted him in Hebrew, saying, "As God blessed you with life in this world, so He will bless you with eternal life." Antiochus suspected that she was cursing him in this language which he did not understand. When the time came for Hannah's youngest son to be executed, Antiochus tried to convince him to deny the God of Israel. When he refused, Antiochus ordered Hannah to persuade the boy and so save her son's life. Finally, she agreed to speak to him. "My son," she said, "go to your death with honor, trusting in God as your brothers did, so that we may all be reunited when the time of redemption comes." The boy turned to Antiochus and said, "We know that though we suffer now, God will yet be merciful with us and has granted us eternal life. But you will suffer greatly for your tyranny, and will never escape divine punishment."

Hannah watched as her youngest son was tortured to death even more cruelly than his brothers. Then she took her own life.

of them vied for his support. With both of them trying to win favor with him, Jonathan was able to expand the territory under his control towards the Mediterranean coast and establish diplomatic relations with Egypt and cities in Greece and Rome.

Jonathan was succeeded by his brother Simeon. By this time, Judea was recognized as an independent nation, and was even exempt from paying taxes to the Seleucid kingdom.

An Independent Judea

When Simeon and two of his sons were assassinated, his third son, John Hyrcanus, became the ruler of Judea. During his reign, the Seleucid kingdom collapsed, and all of the nations in the region, including Judea, were now officially independent. John Hyrcanus considered all of Eretz Yisrael to be the land promised to the Jewish people, and set out to bring it under his control. Gradually he expanded his borders and even forced the Idumeans, who lived within his territory, to convert to Judaism. He also renewed the alliance with Rome, and this was an important stamp of approval for his kingdom.

John Hyrcanus was succeeded by his son, Judah Aristobulus, who died in 103 b.c.e. after only one year on the throne. He was followed by his brother, Alexander Yannai, who continued to expand his territory. However, Alexander Yannai had many enemies, not only among the nations he conquered, but also among his own people, the Jews. The Hasmonean rulers were becoming increasingly like Greek kings. They and their courtiers lived lavishly, they enlarged their army of mercenaries, imposed excessive taxes, and bitterly contended for the throne. They were growing farther and farther apart from much of the nation. Hostility between Alexander and the Pharisees became especially violent. The Pharisees (from the Hebrew word for

17

intervention of Rome in Judea. Within a few years, Pompey led the Roman army into Jerusalem and even into the Temple itself. Pompey revoked Judea's independence. He chose Hyrcanus as ruler, but no longer as king. Instead, in 63 B.C.E. Hyrcanus was appointed high priest and given the title of "ethnarch," a sort of local leader. Judea was now ordered to pay taxes to Rome.

Meanwhile, a new figure was gaining in prominence. This was Herod, who would play an important role in the history of Eretz Yisrael.

16. (On page 64) Palace-like tombs in the Nabatean capital of Petra in Edom, drawn by Roberts in the 19th century.

17. Tombs from the Hasmonean period in the Kidron Valley near Jerusalem.

18. The expansion of the Hasmonean kingdom.

"to interpret" or "explain") were sages who interpreted the Torah (the Law of Moses). Most of the people of the nation lived their daily lives according to their rulings.

There was a short lull in the tension between the two camps during the reign of Queen Salome, who succeeded her husband Alexander Yannai and reigned from 76 to 67 B.C.E. As a woman, Salome could not be high priest, as the other Hasmonean rulers were, so she appointed her son to the post. He won the support of the Pharisees, resulting in fewer conflicts between them and the monarchy. In addition, Salome did not wage many wars, as Alexander had done. In fact, this period is considered in many respects the golden age of the Hasmonean state.

After the death of Salome, her two sons—Aristobulus and Hyrcanus—competed for the throne. They eventually appealed to a foreign power—the Roman general Pompey—to decide between them. By doing so, they invited the open

18

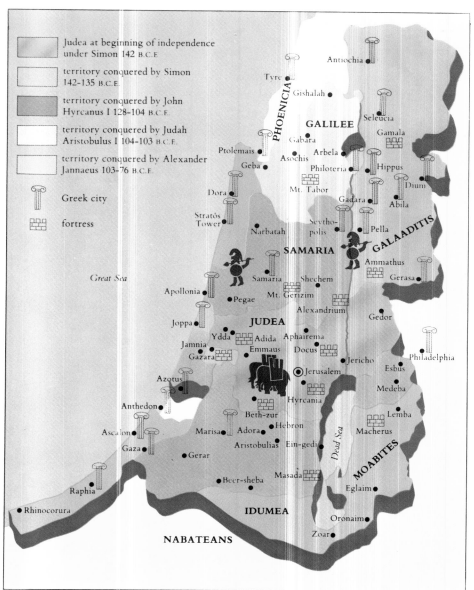

Judea at beginning of independence under Simon 142 B.C.E

territory conquered by Simon 142-135 B.C.E.

territory conquered by John Hyrcanus I 128-104 B.C.E.

territory conquered by Judah Aristobulus I 104-103 B.C.E.

territory conquered by Alexander Jannaeus 103-76 B.C.E.

Greek city

fortress

8 · CULTURE AND RELIGION IN THE SECOND TEMPLE PERIOD

1. An illustration from the Book of Judith, a book of the Apocrypha, from the 15th century Rothschild Manuscript. It tells the story of how Judith, saved a town by beheading the enemy commander, Holofernes. The historical basis of the story is unknown, but some scholars believe it to be an allegory referring to Greek rule.

2. "The heads of the clans of all the people and the priests and Levites gathered to Ezra the scribe to study the words of the Teaching" (Nehemiah 8:13). This depiction of that event was painted by J. Schnor in the early 20th century.

During the period of the Second Temple, described in Chapters 6, 7, and 9, Hellenistic culture—the way of life brought to the region by the Greek rulers—prevailed in Eretz Yisrael. It was during this time that the books of the Hebrew Bible were completed, while the books of the New Testament had not yet been written. Many important works of literature written during this period served as a link not only between the Hebrew Bible and the New Testament, but also between the two cultures—the Jewish and the Hellenistic. In fact, the entire period was dominated by the conflicts between these two civilizations. The centers of Jewish culture at this time were Eretz Yisrael, especially Jerusalem, and Alexandria in Egypt. Alexandria was also the world center of Hellenistic culture.

JUDAISM TAKES FORM

The work of Ezra the scribe in the 5th century B.C.E. brought about the spiritual and cultural unification of the Jewish people in Judah. Both in Eretz Yisrael and beyond, the Jews continued to live according to the sacred words of the *Torah,* the Jewish Law. The many interpretations of the Torah made it possible to apply its

laws to all aspects of daily life. Such commentaries had been framed since the time of the Hasmoneans by sages known as *Tannaim* (from the Aramaic word for "learning" or "repetition"). Much later, in the middle of the 3rd century C.E., these interpretations—known as the Oral Law—were brought together into one book, called the *Mishnah* (also meaning "learning" or "repetition," but in Hebrew).

However, during the Second Temple Period, not everyone agreed about how to interpret the Torah. Different groups suggested different interpretations, and these groups eventually developed into rival sects. Even the rift with the Samaritans, who rejected all standard Jewish standard interpretation of the Torah, grew wider at this time.

The Greek conquest of Eretz Yisrael also brought many Greeks to the region. This was part of the policy of the Hellenistic kings who settled former soldiers in the lands they

religious leadership took shape.

The two dominant schools of Judaism in Eretz Yisrael in the Hellenistic period were the Pharisees and the Sadducees. As we learned in the previous chapter, the name Pharisees probably comes from the Hebrew word *peresh,* meaning "to interpret" or "explain." But some scholars believe it comes from a different source, from the word *parash,* meaning "to be separated," because the Pharisees kept themselves apart from others whom they believed to be unclean. Most of the sages, commentators and teachers of the Torah came from among the

3. The remains of an ancient synagogue from the 3rd century C.E. uncovered at Baram in the Galilee.

4. The remains of a Nabatean town. The Nabateans were tradesmen, and often clashed with the Hasmonean kings.

5. A Nabatean oil lamp of clay decorated with Roman soldiers.

6. "By the king's order, Daniel was then brought and thrown into the lions' den" (Daniel 6:17), in a painting by G. Doré. The story of Daniel is believed to be an allegory for Greek rule in Eretz Yisrael.

3

5

conquered. Thus Greek cities known as *poleis* (*polis* in the singular) were built in Eretz Yisrael and the neighboring lands. The Jews saw these cities as centers of a foreign nation, spreading a religion and culture which did not belong in their land. The Jews also had to withstand the influence of the neighboring nations such as the Idumeans and the Nabateans. Ever since the destruction of the First Temple in 586 B.C.E., the Idumeans had been moving from the East in the direction of Jerusalem, while the Nabateans, a nomadic nation had been settling in the southern regions where the Idumeans had originally lived.

Thus the land was now an arena in which many nations and cultures fought each other, but also influenced each other. It was against this background of cultural diversity that Jewish society and the political strategies of the Jewish national and

6

Pharisees. The majority of the Jews in the outlying towns followed their teachings, although their influence was also great in Jerusalem. The Sadducees (whose name derives from Zadok, the high priest in King David's time) disagreed with the Pharisees in regard to Jewish law. Unlike the Pharisees, the Sadducees interpreted the Torah literally, and did not believe in the eternal life of the soul.

Most of them seem to have come from the upper classes, who had greater contact with Greek culture.

Other smaller sects, such as the Essenes and the "Dead Sea sect," who were believed to be the first Christians, were also active at this time. These sects shared the belief that the Messiah would soon come and herald the redemption of the world according to the vision of the

7. A page from an early manuscript of the Mishnah, which contains the sages' interpretations of the Torah.

8. A view of Edom, the land of the Edomites.

9. The first page of the Book of Ecclesiastes, which was probably written during the Hasmonean period, from the Parma manuscript produced in Italy in the early 14th century.

10. (On page 69) The Menorah, a seven-branched candelabra, was an early symbol of Judaism recalling the Menorah in the Temple. This one is part of the mosaic floor of an ancient synagogue found in Maon by the Sea of Galilee.

11. (On page 69) The caves in which the Dead Sea Scrolls were found.

12. (On page 69) One of the clay jars in which the Dead Sea Scrolls were found.

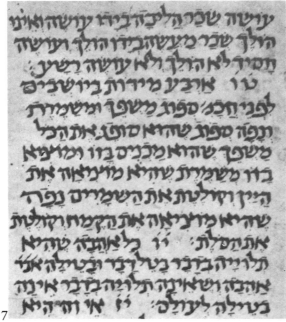

7

9

8

prophets. They also believed that there was a predetermined divine plan for redemption and that certain people, chosen by God, could discover this plan.

Jewish Literature in Eretz Yisrael

The belief in the redemption gave birth to a great deal of literature whose major purpose was to discover when and how the redemption would come. One example is the Book of Daniel in the Hebrew Bible. Some parts of the book contain a prediction of the time of the redemption. Other writings that tried to calculate this date were confiscated by the dominant Jewish groups, but the members of the minority sects continued to consider them sacred. One of the ways these books were made to appear holy was by a clever literary ruse. The author would not identify himself, but would pretend to be a famous figure of antiquity, like Adam, one of the sons of Jacob, Moses, David, Solomon, Jeremiah, and others. Literature of this kind is called "pseudepigrapha," from the Greek word for "fake."

Not all of the literature written at the time concerned the coming of the Messiah. Many books of the type that

10

appear in the Hebrew Bible were also written. There were psalms like those in the Book of Psalms, proverbs like the ones in the Book of Proverbs, and books that recorded the history of the period, like the historical books of Kings and Deuteronomy. One of the books written early in this period is Ecclesiastes, whose author presents himself as the son of David, King of Jerusalem (although this too is an example of pseudepigrapha). The book begins with these eternal words:

"One generation goes, another comes
But the earth remains the same forever.
The sun rises and the sun sets—
And glides back to where it rises...
Only that shall happen
Which has happened,
Only that occur
Which has occurred;
There is nothing new
Beneath the sun!" (1:4-9)

THE DEAD SEA SCROLLS

On a broiling hot day in the summer of 1947, a young Bedouin boy was grazing his goats near the ruins of Qumran by the Dead Sea. Looking for a bit of shade, he entered one of the many caves in the rock wall. Having nothing else to do, he tossed pebbles deep into the cave. From the sound they made, the young boy, Muhammed ed Dib, realized that they had struck something. He went to investigate, and found several large covered clay jars. When he looked inside, he found that they held rolled-up pieces of parchment. Muhammed took the parchment to the shoemaker for a pair of new sandals. The shoemaker immediately saw that there was more than the makings of sandals here.

This was how the famous Dead Sea Scrolls were first discovered. When Muhammed's parchments reached the hands of scholars, it became clear just how important they were. The local Bedouins began searching in the Qumran caves. They found more scrolls and fragments of scrolls. They contained handwritten parts of the books of the Hebrew Bible—the oldest copies ever found of books of the Apocrypha, and of previously unknown works that were the writings of the religious community that lived here. They dated from the 1st century B.C.E. to the 1st century C.E.

Despite the large amount of information in the scrolls, there are still many unanswered questions about the size and history of this sect and its relations with other communities. Were these the Essenes mentioned by Josephus?

One of the mysteries concerns a scroll written on a thin sheet of copper. It contains a list of places, a sort of pirate's map, describing where the treasures of the Temple were hidden:

"...three miles northeast, under the tree, near the well, a cave. There 400 talents of gold.... 40 steps from the ruins, near the valley, in a hole, under the wall, to the east in the rock, jugs of silver 600, and under the big threshold 16 feet deep in the ground 40 talents of silver.... In the hole under the stairs 42 talents of gold..."

Is this just invention, or does it actually record the hiding places of a real treasure? Anyone who could decipher the riddle of the map and find this buried treasure, could surely live in luxury for the rest of his life.

11

12

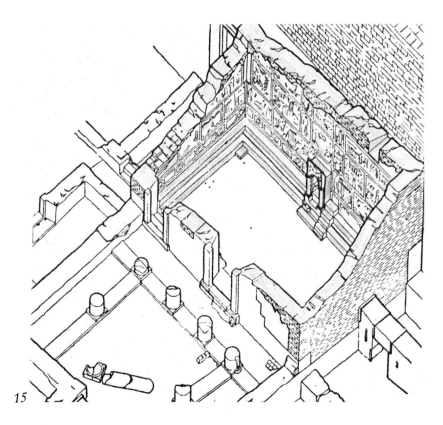

13. Jewish folk art reflected the longing to return to Jerusalem. Papercuts with a Menorah representing the Temple were hung on the wall of the synagogue. This papercut was made in North Africa in the 19th century.

14. A papercut showing a Menorah and the Tablets of the Law made in Poland in the 19th century.

Among other books from this time that have survived are those that tell the history of the period. One of these is the Book of Maccabees which relates the history of the Hasmonean revolt and kingdom. This book, too, was preserved only in Greek. Two other very important books, called *Jewish Antiquities* and *The Jewish War,* were written by Josephus Flavius, or Joseph son of Mattathias, one of the

leaders of the revolt against the Romans described in Chapter 9. His books are our major source of information about the events that took place during the Greek and Roman periods in Eretz Yisrael.

JEWISH LITERATURE OUTSIDE ERETZ YISRAEL

The political independence of Judea, its thriving cultural life, and the importance of the Temple in Jerusalem all enhanced the status of Eretz Yisrael among the Jews living beyond its borders, in what is known as the Diaspora (anywhere outside of Eretz Yisrael where Jews live). Every year, especially on the festival of Passover, tens of thousands of Jews from Babylon, Egypt, Greece, Italy, and the coastal towns of Asia Minor (Turkey today) would gather in Jerusalem. The Land of Israel, and particularly Jerusalem, became the center of the entire Jewish nation, and an extensive network of links grew up between it and the Diaspora. Many Diaspora Jews sent their sons to Jerusalem to study the Torah. Thus the Jews in the Diaspora felt a part of what was happening in Jerusalem, and during the Hasmonean period

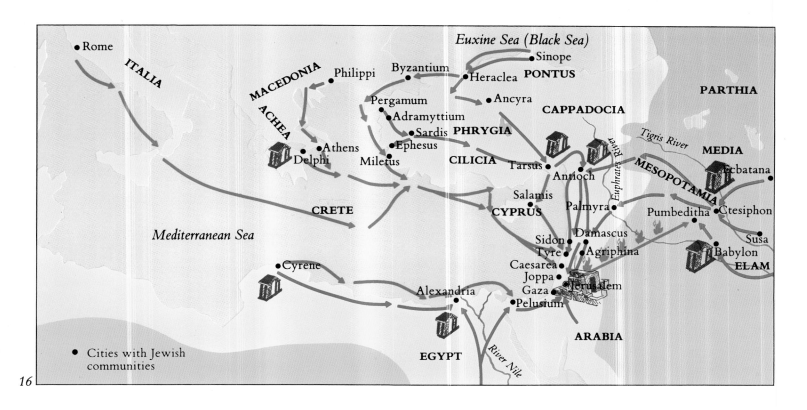

Euxine Sea (Black Sea)

Rome
ITALIA
MACEDONIA
Philippi
Byzantium
Heraclea
Sinope
PONTUS
PARTHIA
ACHEA
Pergamum
Ancyra
CAPPADOCIA
Adramyttium
Sardis
PHRYGIA
MEDIA
Athens
Ephesus
Tigris River
Delphi
Miletus
CILICIA
Tarsus
Antioch
MESOPOTAMIA
Ecbatana
CRETE
Salamis
Palmyra
Ctesiphon
CYPRUS
Pumbeditha
Mediterranean Sea
Sidon
Damascus
Susa
Tyre
Agriphina
Caesarea
Babylon
Cyrene
Joppa
Jerusalem
ELAM
Alexandria
Gaza
Pelusium
ARABIA
Cities with Jewish
communities
EGYPT
River Nile

16

even the rulers in Rome consulted the local Jews in regard to their policies in Jerusalem.

One of the ways in which Diaspora Jews showed their connection with Eretz Yisrael was by donating one half *shekel* every year to the Temple in Jerusalem. This practice, which began in the Hasmonean period, was even adopted by many advocates of the Jews who never actually converted to Judaism themselves. In addition, wealthy Jews often donated much larger amounts, primarily to the Temple. With the help of such a donation from a rich Alexandrian Jew, one of the gates of the Temple was built, and in his honor it was called the Nicanor Gate. Another

large contribution from the Jews of Alexandria enabled the gates of the Temple to be plated in gold.

These links between the Jews in the Diaspora and Jerusalem helped to bring the fame of the city to all corners of the Roman Empire, and not only among the Jews. This fact played an important role many years later when Jesus's disciples journeyed from Jerusalem to spread the word of Christianity beyond the borders of the Land of Israel.

Nevertheless, the central status of Jerusalem did not prevent the Jews from carrying on extensive cultural activities wherever they lived, and most notably in Alexandria, Egypt. The Jews of Egypt felt a constant need to prove to the Hellenistic world around them that they, too, had a highly developed culture. Most of the literature written there contained commentaries, legends, and philosophical discussions relating to the Bible. Beyond a doubt, the most important cultural achievement of the time was the translation of the Hebrew Bible into Greek, a project also undertaken in Egypt. It was begun in the 3rd century B.C.E. and completed about 100 years later.

15. (On page 70) A reconstruction of the most ancient synagogue found outside of Eretz Yisrael, at Dura Europos on the Euphrates River, from as early as the 3rd century. Its walls were painted with scenes from the Bible.

16. Pilgrimages to Eretz Yisrael from the Jewish communities outside the country during the period of the Second Temple, illustrating the central importance of Jerusalem. The status of the city was so great that the Jewish calendar was determined there, and the information passed on to Babylon by a series of torches lit on mountain tops.

17. The port of Alexandria in Egypt as a Jewish delegation returns to the city from Rome, in a reconstruction in the Museum of the Jewish Diaspora in Tel Aviv.

17

The Qumran Community

One of the religious communities in Eretz Yisrael lived at Qumran by the Dead Sea. The Dead Sea Scrolls tell us much about the beliefs of this unusual community. Some scholars believe that they were the Essenes mentioned by Josephus Flavius in his books.

The members of this sect believed that the Messiah would appear very soon, and their interpretation of the Bible was determined by this belief. They thought that before the time of redemption came, there would be a terrible war between "the sons of light"—the members of the sect—and "the sons of darkness"—who included not only the Roman conquerors, but anyone who did not belong to their community, both Jews and non-Jews alike. As a result, they were in constant conflict with the major schools of Jewish thought, which naturally did not adopt their beliefs. The leader of the sect was known as the "Teacher of Righteousness," and was thought to be a man of God. It was probably he who wrote their hymns of thanksgiving. The members of the sect lived a communal life. They owned no private property and occupied themselves mainly with copying out manuscripts of the books of the Bible and their own special rules.

The scroll containing the rules of the community begins with these words: "For the man of understanding that He may instruct the saints to live according to the rule of the community; to see God with all their heart and all their soul and so what is good and right before Him... and to love all that He had chosen and hate all that He despised..."

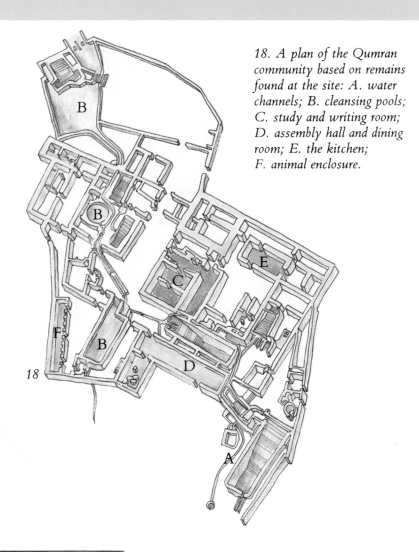

18. A plan of the Qumran community based on remains found at the site: A. water channels; B. cleansing pools; C. study and writing room; D. assembly hall and dining room; E. the kitchen; F. animal enclosure.

According to the tradition of Alexandrian Jews, King Ptolemy invited 72 elders of Jerusalem to Egypt. He placed each of them on a separate island in the Nile River, and there they translated the Torah, the first five books of the Bible. When they were through, the 72 translations were compared and found to be exactly alike. This tradition shows the reverence with which the Jews of Egypt regarded this initial translation of the Torah, which was the first stage in the translation of the entire Hebrew Bible. It is known as the Septuagint, the "translation of the 70."

Other books were also translated into Greek. Some were pseude-pigraphs, and some had been confiscated by the religious leaders in Eretz Yisrael but were regarded as sacred by the Jews of Egypt and were included in the Septuagint. These books are called Apocrypha, from the Greek for "to hide away." For the first time, these translations made it possible for the Hellenists to read the ideas of people who believed in one God. Indeed, during this period many people throughout the east converted to Judaism, won over by the Jewish belief in monotheism as an alternative to a belief in many gods.

The fact that so many civilizations were in close contact at this time also had great significance for the future. It prepared the groundwork for Christianity to take over the Hellenistic world, a process that began in Eretz Yisrael.

9 · KING HEROD AND ROMAN RULE

The mighty Roman Empire first began to play a role in Eretz Yisrael at the start of the Hasmonean revolt in the 2nd century B.C.E. Slowly but surely, it expanded its influence until Eretz Yisrael had become a Roman province. And as its influence grew, so opposition to the new rulers grew too. The first of these rulers was Herod.

KING HEROD

Herod was the son of Antipater, a powerful minister in the court of John Hyrcanus. Antipater was an Idumean who converted to Judaism. He offered Rome his enthusiastic support. In return, one of his sons, Phasael, was appointed governor of Jerusalem, and another, Herod, was made governor of the Galilee.

Herod ruled the Galilee with an iron hand, and was deeply hated by the Jews there. Opposition to him was so strong, that he was forced to flee to Rome. There he convinced the Roman senate that he was much more loyal to Rome than any of the Hasmoneans. He suggested that he be made ruler of Jerusalem on Rome's behalf. Thus Herod was appointed "King of Jerusalem." He returned to Eretz Yisrael at the head of an army of mercenaries and Roman soldiers, and conquered large parts of the country. After three years of war he marched on Jerusalem, placed a siege around the city, and forced it to surrender. In the year 37 B.C.E., Herod assumed the throne of Jerusalem.

The leaders of Rome considered

1. Coins from King Herod's time. The king's large income came from the heavy taxes he imposed on the people, from customs, and from Hasmonean properties which fell into his hands. He used this money to finance his spectacular building projects and the bribes and generous gifts he gave to powerful Romans.

2. The expansion of Herod's kingdom.

1

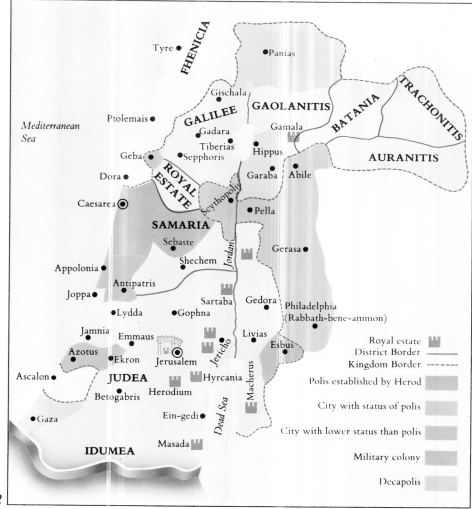

2

3. King Herod's palace at Masada, near the Dead Sea.

4. Herod's mountaintop fortress of Herodium near Bethlehem also served as a palace.

5. Part of an aqueduct built by Herod at Caesarea to channel fresh water to the city. The king spent huge sums of money to construct this city and its port.

Herod the perfect governor, calling him Herod the Great. They returned to his control lands that had been taken away from John Hyrcanus, and Herod himself expanded his kingdom even more. Indeed, he was one of the greatest builders in the history of Eretz Yisrael. He erected dozens of fine buildings, and fortified cities and palaces. His most ambitious project was the renovation of Jerusalem and the Temple. Jerusalem became one of the most magnificent cities in the East.

When Herod became king, Jewish hatred of him grew even stronger—he was referred to as Herod the Wicked. First, he was remembered for the cruelty and bloodshed of his rule of the Galilee. Secondly, he himself was not a Hasmonean, although his wife Mariamne was. And thirdly, more than any governor before him, he drew his power from Rome and was therefore considered to be a foreign ruler, especially because his family was originally Idumean. Moreover, Herod ruled in the spirit of the Hellenistic Roman culture, whereas the Hasmonean kings had been committed to Jewish culture and religion.

During Herod's reign, in the midst of uprisings and conflicts over the very fate of the nation and the land, an event took place that few people at the time were aware of. But it was to prove one of the most important

3

4

HEROD'S BLOODY REIGN

An example of Herod's ruthlessness towards anyone he imagined might conceivably pose a threat to his authority can be found in the New Testament. It is part of the traditions surrounding the birth of Jesus (which we will consider at greater length in Chapter 10).

Matthew relates that when Jesus was born in Bethlehem, a rumor began to spread that the King of the Jews had been born. When Herod heard of this, he sent emissaries to the town to find the baby, but they warned Jesus's father and the family fled to Egypt. "Then Herod, when he saw that he was mocked... was exceeding wroth, and sent forth, and slew all the children that were in Bethlehem, and in all the coasts thereof, from two years old and under" (Matthew 2:16).

5

events in the history of the world. A son was born to Joseph and Mary, a Jewish couple from Nazareth in the Galilee. According to Christian tradition, he was born in Bethlehem, near Jerusalem.

JESUS OF NAZARETH

Our knowledge of the life of Jesus comes from the accounts of his apostles which are contained in the New Testament. Like other stories of a nation's ancestors, of prophets and of men of God, these accounts include reports of miraculous events. Some people believe these things happened just as they are told, while others try to find the historical truth behind them. That is something which everyone must decide for himself. What we shall do here is to draw the historical picture which emerges from the Gospels, the name for the books of the New Testament in which four of Jesus's apostles—Matthew, Luke, Mark, and John—tell of the life of Jesus.

Jesus lived in Nazareth, but he traveled widely throughout the Galilee and often journeyed to Jerusalem for the festivals. He could not bear the poverty and suffering he saw all around him, while at the same time the privileged classes—the priests, tax collectors, and courtiers—lived rich and pampered lives. His heart went out to the simple people, to the farmers, the fishermen, and the incurably ill. When Jesus was about 30 years old, he joined with John the Baptist, another Jewish preacher who lived on the banks of the Jordan River. John called on the Jews to repent and to immerse themselves in the waters of the Jordan as a sign of the new life they would promise to lead.

Jesus spent some time in the Judean Desert, and then returned to Nazareth where he began to preach his beliefs. He did not speak against Judaism, but against the Pharisees' interpretations

of the Bible and its laws. According to Jesus, in the eyes of God people's relations with their fellow men and women were more important than their proper performance of the ritual. The greatest virtues were faith in God, love of God and of all human beings, modesty, and humility. Although this was not much different from what many of the Pharisees themselves preached, Jesus was regarded as something of a revolutionary, and was deeply distrusted by the Pharisees.

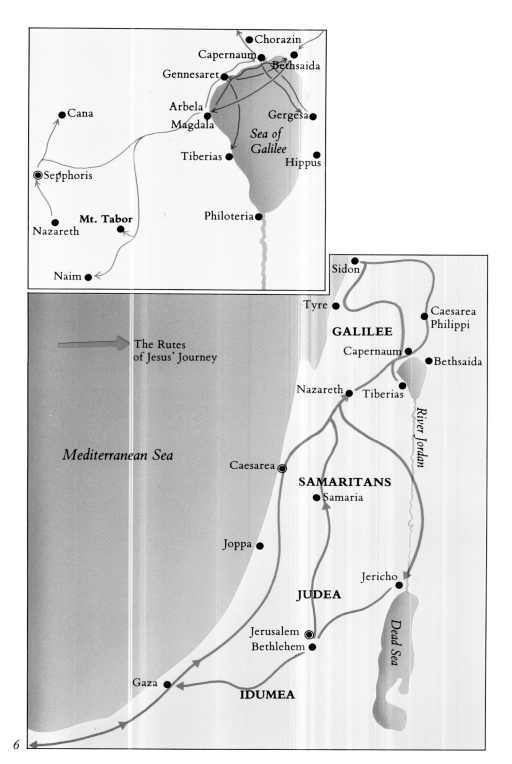

6. According to Christian tradition, these are the places Jesus visited on his journeys throughout Eretz Yisrael and Egypt.

7

8

9

7. Jesus and Mary on a 16th century icon (a religious object of Eastern Christians) from Crete. It is part of the huge collection of icons at the Santa Katerina monastery in the Sinai, one of the oldest Christian monasteries in the world.

8. Jesus washing the feet of his disciples, part of an ivory relief at the Duomo Cathedral in Milan.

9. The evidence of Pontius Pilate's rule as procurator of Judea was found on a stone bearing his name that was uncovered during excavations of the amphitheater at Caesarea.

KING HEROD AND ROMAN RULE

Jesus continued to preach throughout Eretz Yisrael. He spoke before Jews, Samaritans, and even Greeks. His apostles tell of his aid to the poor, of miracles he performed, of curing the hopelessly ill, and of how he gave even the most unfortunate souls the feeling that God had not forsaken them. On the contrary, their suffering, he claimed, brought them closer to God than those who enjoyed the luxuries of this world. Man, said Jesus, would receive his true reward in heaven, at the time of redemption in the End of Days.

Jesus attracted more and more followers, but until his death they were still only a very small group. Who would have believed that before many years had passed they would swell until a new religion had been born—Christianity.

At the age of about 33, Jesus went to Jerusalem for the Passover festival. His followers joined him on the journey. The Gospels do not agree as to exactly what happened in Jerusalem, and so it is difficult for us to be sure of the events that took

place there. It would seem that Jesus went to the Temple and drove away the peddlers and money changers who sought out customers among the worshipers. He entered into harsh debates with the priests, infuriating them. They were particularly upset because Jesus's followers regarded him as a messianic figure and listened to him rather than to the dictates of the religious establishment.

The Roman authorities also objected to this picture of Jesus as the Messiah. They feared that messianic movements would lead to rebellion. Jesus was informed on by Judas Iscariot, one of his apostles. On the orders of the Roman procurator, Pontius Pilate, he was arrested and put to death by crucifixion. The Roman soldiers made fun of his claim to be the "king of the Jews," pressing a crown of thorns on his head.

According to Christian belief, Jesus was resurrected on the third day after his crucifixion. He appeared before his apostles, chided them for their lack of faith, and told them to spread his word throughout the world.

Even after the death of Jesus, (who considered himself a Jew), his followers considered themselves Jews. But there was one crucial difference between them and the rest of the nation. While other Jews continued to await the coming of the Messiah, Jesus's followers believed he had already come.

HEROD'S SUCCESSORS

Herod died in the year 4 B.C.E. and his kingdom was divided up among his children: Antipas was given control of the Galilee and the Transjordan; Philip received the Golan, the Bashan, and the Hula Valley; Salome was given territory on the Mediterranean coast; and Archelaus was named King of Judea, although Rome took the title of king away from him.

After Archelaus had ruled for ten years, during which time he seems to

have continued his father's policies, he was removed from power by Rome. Rome now divided all of its empire into provinces, each ruled by a Roman governor, known as a procurator.

The procurators governed Eretz Yisrael for 35 years (6-41 A.D.—we now begin counting the years after the birth of Christ, as we do today). Most of them were concerned with running the economic and political affairs of their province, and did not interfere in the cultural and religious life. The most famous procurator— Pontius Pilate—was an exception to this rule. The Jews considered some of his edicts to be serious offenses to the Temple and to their freedom of worship. Riots broke out in the land, and they were brutally suppressed by Pontius Pilate. New religious movements began to claim that the Messiah would soon appear and rescue the nation from oppression.

There was a short break in the rule of the procurators between the years 41 and 44. Herod's grandson, Agrippa, lived in Rome and had excellent contacts in the imperial court. He had even succeeded in settling certain internal disputes there. In appreciation, he was appointed king of all of Eretz Yisrael. The fact that Agrippa was also the grandson of Mariamne, Herod's Hasmonean wife, brought him the favor of the Jewish population. Some people even hoped that Jerusalem would again become the capital of an independent Jewish kingdom. But when Agrippa died only a short time after becoming king, this hope was dashed.

The Great Revolt

In the year 66, the Jews rebelled against Rome in what is known as the Great Revolt. There were a number of causes for the uprising. First, the procurators who ruled Judea were cruel and corrupt. Again and again they raised the taxes, placing an especially heavy burden on the villagers. Secondly, in the cities where both Jews and non-Jews lived, particularly in Caesaria, the different sectors of the population clashed repeatedly with one another as each tried to promote its own culture. When such incidents occurred, the Romans naturally ruled against the

10. *"In the place where he was crucified there was a garden; and in the garden a new sepulcher.... There laid they Jesus" (John 19:41-42). The garden tomb in Jerusalem where, according to Christian tradition, Jesus was buried.*

11. *A Roman soldier dressed for battle.*

11

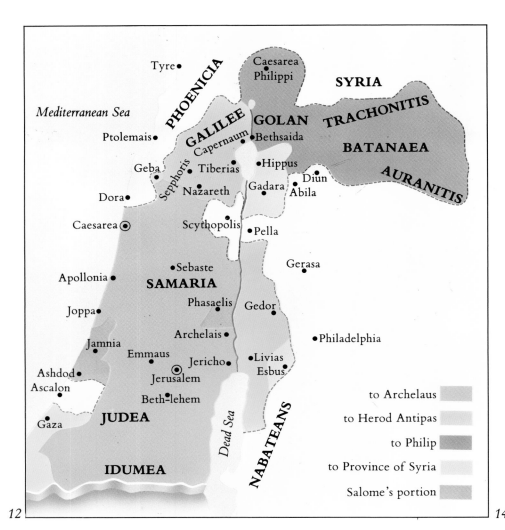

both Jews and Romans alike.

During Passover in the year 66, when thousands of people had gathered in Jerusalem for the festival, riots broke out in the city. The Roman soldiers quelled the riots, spilling much blood. They even broke into the Temple and plundered its treasures. This enraged the population even more, and the revolt spread throughout the country. A group of zealots destroyed the Roman garrison at Masada, and took control of this mountain fortress in the Judean Desert. From here the rebels set out

Jews and in favor of the Hellenists.

Thirdly, the idea that the Messiah would soon come had won many followers among the Jews. A large part of the nation believed that a rebellion against Rome, even if it was not immediately successful, would be the first stage in the war that would end in the redemption of the world. And so, as Roman rule became more and more oppressive, increasing numbers of people joined the rebels, known as "zealots."

Bands of zealots went into hiding in the desert areas around Jerusalem. From time to time they would launch a raid against a town whose inhabitants opposed the revolt. A band of particularly violent rebels, known as *Sicarii* (from the Greek word for "knife"), operated in Jerusalem itself. They got their name from the short knives they carried concealed under their cloaks. They used them to murder their political opponents—

for Jerusalem, killing a large number of Roman soldiers on their way. In the mixed cities, the Jews and non-Jews warred against each other, with many casualties on both sides.

A national council was set up in Jerusalem to organize the rebellion. It appointed commanders for the various sections of the country. The commanders both organized the warriors in their region and looked

12. *Herod's kingdom was divided up among his heirs.*

13. *The helmet of a Roman horseman found in Israel.*

14. *Clay utensils found among the ruins of a Jewish house in Jerusalem from the time of the Revolt against the Romans.*

15. *One of the earliest synagogues in Eretz Yisrael was erected on Masada.*

after the needs of the local population.

In the year 67, the Roman emperor Nero sent Vespasian, one of his senior generals, to put down the revolt. Vespasian set out for Judea at the head of an army of 60,000 soldiers. Their first campaign was to place a siege around the city of Jotapata where the commander of the Galilee, Josephus ben Matthias (Josephus Flavius), had his headquarters. The city was captured and its inhabitants brutally murdered. Josephus managed to escape with 40 of his men. Later, he defected to the Romans. The Great Revolt is described in detail, from Josephus's perspective, in his book *The Jewish War*. One by one, the towns of the Galilee fell to the Romans. The Jewish soldiers needed more than just their faith and bravery to defeat the might of the Roman army.

The strength of the Roman army was only one of the causes for the fall of the Galilee, however. Another was the internal conflicts among the Jews themselves. Not everyone accepted the leadership of Josephus, for example. Bickering among the zealots, moderates, Sicarii and others also plagued Jerusalem and prevented coordination among the different groups of rebels in the city.

In the year 69, Vespasian became the new Roman emperor. He delegated the task of conquering Jerusalem to his son, Titus. The following year, having been under siege for five months, the city surrendered. The Temple was burned to the ground, and only the western section of the wall of the outer courtyard remained standing. To this day, on the ninth day of the Hebrew month of Ab (July/August), Jews fast and mourn the destruction of the Temple in the year 70. The small section of the wall that was not destroyed still stands. It is known as the Western or Wailing Wall, and remains a sacred site for Jews to this day.

Thus the Great Revolt was

JOSEPHUS FLAVIUS

Quite a lot is known about the Jewish historian Josephus Flavius, who lived from 37 to 100 A.D. He was one of the most fascinating figures in the Hellenistic period, and in many ways he symbolizes the conflict between Judaism and Hellenism.

Josephus came from an important family of priests from Jerusalem, and was descended from the Hasmoneans on his mother's side. He was a very intelligent person who was well-versed in the interpretations of the Pharisees, highly curious about the other Jewish sects, and eager to learn as much as he could about Hellenistic culture. At the age of 26, he was sent by the Jewish community of Jerusalem on a mission to Rome. He was so deeply influenced by the culture he found there that it affected the rest of his life. When the Jews rebelled against Rome in the year 67, Josephus was appointed commander of the Galilee. While under siege in Jotapata, he decided that the revolt had no chance of success, and deserted his soldiers to go over to the Romans. During the revolt, Josephus tried to convince his fellow Jews to surrender to Rome, but he was considered a traitor and ignored.

When Jerusalem was conquered and the Second Temple destroyed in the year 70 A.D., Josephus moved to Rome. There he wrote his books: *Jewish Antiquities, The Jewish War*, his autobiography *The Life of Josephus Flavius,* and *Against Apion*, a defense of the Jews against the harsh attacks of one of the Hellenistic scholars. Josephus, like every true historian, was interested in the truth, and so it is from his own books that we learn of his betrayal. In fact, we owe much of what we know about the Hellenistic period in Eretz Yisrael to Josephus—although many contemporary historians say he wrote with a pro-Roman bias.

16

suppressed, although the zealots remained in control of two fortresses, Machaerus and Masada. It took the Romans three years to capture Masada. When it was clear they could no longer hold out against the

16. Masada, the fortress built by Herod on a steep cliff near the Dead Sea, was the last stronghold of the rebels defying Rome.

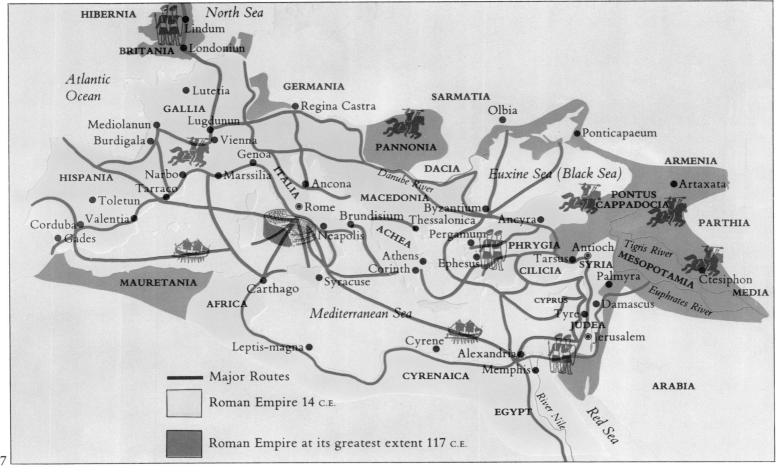

17. *The Roman Empire in the 1st century C.E.*

18. *Roman soldiers were towed to the scene of battle in this "troop carrier," and then could jump out, fresh and ready to meet the enemy.*

18

Romans, the Jews left on Masada died by their own hand, rather than be taken alive by their enemy. Since then, Masada has been a symbol of heroism and courage.

The rebels at Masada were led by the Sicari, Eleazar ben Yair. In one of the most moving sections of his book, Josephus Flavius describes their last moments, quoting from Eleazar's words to the warriors:

Long since, my brave companions, we determined to serve neither the Romans nor anyone else but only God, for He alone is the true and righteous Lord of men; now the time has come that bids us prove our resolution by our deeds.... Up to now we have never submitted to slavery.... Let our wives die undishonored and our children without knowing slavery; and when they are gone let us do each other an ungrudging kindness, preserving our liberty as a noble funeral monument.... Let us spare only one thing—our store of food; for it will

testify when we are dead, that we did not perish through want but because, in keeping with our initial resolution, we chose death to slavery.

AFTER THE DEFEAT

When Jerusalem fell, bringing an end to the revolt, thousands of Jews were deported from Judea and the Galilee. They were taken to Rome, Cyrene (Libya), Salonika, Crete, and North Africa. Many were sold into slavery. However, in the regions where the fighting had not been fierce—in the Galilee (parts of which were quiet after the surrender), southern Judea, the coastal plain, and the Jordan Valley—most of the Jewish population was allowed to remain. The Romans gave their support to the more moderate leaders, but did not interfere in the social and religious life of the Jews.

The Romans now wished to improve the economy, which had suffered greatly during the revolt. They strengthened the Hellenist cities, and Jews too were allowed to live in them. But Jerusalem was no longer a Jewish city. The cultural center of the Pharisees, now the dominant stream in Judaism both in and beyond Eretz Yisrael, moved to Jabneh. The leader of the community there was Rabban Johanan ben Zakkai. He was the head of the *Sanhedrin,* the supreme judicial and religious institution of the Jews. Rabban ben Zakkai was a Pharisee sage from Jerusalem who had harshly opposed the revolt. He left Jerusalem, hidden in a coffin, even before the city fell, and received permission from the Romans to transfer the Sanhedrin to Jabneh.

Now that the Temple had been destroyed, the synagogues became the center of religious life. People not only prayed here, but also studied the Torah and debated its interpretation. The nation's leaders had learned their lesson from the bickering among the different sects before the defeat of Jerusalem. They now banished anyone who disagreed with the Pharisee interpretations of the Law. For many years the whole of the Hebrew Bible had been considered a sacred book which could no longer be altered in any way. This attitude was officially sanctioned in Jabneh. No additional writings could ever become part of the Jewish Holy Scriptures.

Despite the failure of the revolt and the new emphasis on spirituality and study of the Torah, the Jews did not cease to await the coming of the Messiah. Both in Eretz Yisrael and beyond, many continued to believe that redemption would soon come and they would be free of subjection to Rome. A small group of people believed the Messiah had already appeared, in the person of Jesus of Nazareth.

THE BAR KOKHBA REVOLT

The first Jews to rebel against Rome after the Great Revolt did not live in Eretz Yisrael, but in the Diaspora (the name for all Jewish settlement outside of Eretz Yisrael). An uprising took place in Cyrene in the year 116. It was led by Lucuas, who many Jews believed to be the Messiah. The rebellion spread to Alexandria in Egypt, gaining more and more support from the Jews in the Nile

19

20

Valley and Delta. A similar uprising broke out in Cyprus. The following year, the Jews of Babylon and Hadiab joined the revolt against Rome. All of these rebellions were put down. Their most tragic consequence was the annihilation of most of the Jews of Egypt, outside of Alexandria.

19. *The entrance to a cave near Hebron used by Bar Kokhba's warriors. They could remain in hiding for many months in the extensive network of caves in the area.*

20. *A bronze head of the Roman emperor Hadrian found in Israel. It was probably sculpted during the time of the Bar Kokhba revolt.*

21

22

21. *This coin, minted in honor of the dedication of Jerusalem as a pagan Roman city, bears the words "the colony of Aelia Capitolina is founded," and the depiction of an ancient Roman rite celebrated at the founding of a city. The emperor is seen plowing with a bull and a cow, with the furrow marking the future borders of the city.*

22. *The rebels hurled these stones down on the Romans.*

23

24

25

start of the revolt, he collected the money needed to finance it, and sent Rabbi Akiva out to the Jewish communities in the Diaspora to gather their contributions as well. He convinced the Samaritans and other nations of low social and economic

23. The Emperor Titus thanked the gods for his victory over the Jews by placing idols in this Greek temple to the god Pan near the source of the River Jordan.

24. A letter written on papyrus by Simeon Bar Kokhba to one of his generals, concerning the supply of wheat to the warriors.

25. A Roman milestone found in Jerusalem.

In the year 130, the Roman emperor Hadrian decided to establish a Roman colony in Jerusalem. The Jews in Eretz Yisrael were deeply disturbed by this plan. They feared they would never be allowed to rebuild the Temple in Jerusalem. Tempers rose, and another revolt broke out.

Little is known about this revolt, as compared to the extensive information we have about the Great Revolt or the Hasmonean period. What we do know comes from the Roman historian Dio Cassius (2nd-3rd centuries), from Jewish religious literature, and from archeological finds which are still being uncovered even today.

The leader of the revolt was Simeon ben Kosiba, also known as Bar Kokhba ("son of a star"). He was greatly admired and many legends were told about him. Rabbi Akiva, one of the most prominent sages at the time, called him the Messiah. He had the total support of most of the nation. Bar Kokhba was an excellent organizer. He learned the lessons of the Great Revolt and tried to avoid making the same mistakes. Before the

status to join with the Jews against the Romans. In this way, the revolt became a social, as well as a national, uprising.

The revolt broke out near Modi'in, the village of Mattathias the Hasmonean, in the year 131. The Roman army was taken completely by surprise. They withdrew their soldiers from Jerusalem, and the city again became the capital of the Jewish state. Coins were minted as a symbol of national independence. They bore dates such as: "Year 1 of the Redemption of Israel," and "Year 2 of the Liberty of Israel," and "Simeon Bar Kokhba was declared President of Israel."

The revolt had begun in Judea. Bar Kokhba attempted to extend it to the Galilee, but he could not win the support of the majority of the Jewish population there.

In the meantime, Rome was amassing a huge army in Eretz Yisrael, gathering its forces from throughout its great empire. However, they did not attempt to defeat Bar Kokhba in one decisive battle. Instead the Roman generals

26

waged smaller battles wherever they had a clear advantage. Using this strategy, they captured the cities and towns around Jerusalem from the rebels. It was now time to conquer the capital itself. Jerusalem fell in the fourth year of the revolt. Only one stronghold remained in the hands of Bar Kokhba and his warriors—the city of Betar to the southwest of Jerusalem. When Betar fell, the revolt was nearly over.

Bar Kokhba fled with his men and their families to the Judean Desert where they hid in the many caves in the rock walls. From there they launched desperate raids on the Romans. We know much about their life in the desert from the many letters, documents, and objects found in these caves. Bar Kokhba was more than just their general. It was he, for example, who made sure they had food, which was brought from the eastern Transjordan or from supplies prepared before the fall of Jerusalem. Nevertheless, all of the people died of starvation or were burnt to death when the Romans placed a siege around their caves. From the bones,

27

artifacts, and letters found in one of the caves, it is clear that in the fourth year of the revolt, the inhabitants of the region still gave their full allegiance to Bar Kokhba.

Hundreds of thousands of Jews lost their lives in the revolt and were sold into slavery. From that time on, the Jews constituted a minority in Eretz Yisrael.

To this day historians disagree about Bar Kokhba. Did he take a

26. Bar Kokhba's warriors brought their families with them to the caves in the Judean Desert. These copper utensils were found in a basket in one of the caves.

27. These objects, found in a basket in a cave in the Judean Desert, belonged to one of the women hiding there along with Bar Kokhba and his warriors.

28

29

28. *Dozens of synagogues were erected in the Land of Israel after the destruction of the Second Temple. This is a reconstruction of one of them, built in the Galilee in the north. Jews continued to live in this region for many generations.*

29. *Part of the mosaic floor of a synagogue found near Jericho by the Dead Sea. It contains a Menorah—an ancient Jewish symbol—and the words "Peace over Israel."*

hopeless risk that had tragic results for the Jewish people, or was there a chance of success for his revolt? Did it bring honor to the nation, proving that despite their small numbers the Jews preferred to rise up against the might of Rome rather than deny their religious and cultural principles? Jewish tradition tells of ten religious scholars, among them Rabbi Akiva, who were tortured and burnt to death by the Romans. The memory of these martyrs, known as the "Ten Victims of the Empire," gave courage to Jews throughout the generations who were forced to die for their beliefs.

THE MISHNAH AND THE TALMUD

Once the Bar Kokhba revolt was quelled, Jerusalem became a Roman city by the name of Aelia Capitolina. Jews were no longer allowed to live there. However, a Jewish community remained in Eretz Yisrael in the Galilee. The Sanhedrin continued to function, although it moved from one Galilean town to another. With the consent of Rome, the head of the Sanhedrin (whose title was *nasi*) was given official status and broad judicial authority over the Jewish community.

One of the most celebrated men to hold this post was Rabbi Judah ha-Nasi (135-220), who was known simply as "Rabbi." Judah ha-Nasi was not only a great religious sage, but also a wealthy man who conducted extensive international trade. He was on friendly terms with the Roman emperor, Caracalla, who granted him lands throughout Eretz Yisrael. Thus, Rabbi Judah ha-Nasi was regarded almost as a president by the Jews, and it was this status that enabled him to undertake his greatest project: the compilation of the Mishnah.

For hundreds of years, Jewish scholars and sages had studied and interpreted the Torah. These religious debates were known as the Oral Law, and had never been written down in any organized fashion. Rabbi Judah ha-Nasi realized that all of this material had to be collected and arranged so that Jews all over the world would have a single book on which the rabbis and religious judges could base their rulings.

Ever since the completion of the Mishnah, it has served as the basic book of Jewish law. The Talmud, completed several hundred years later, contains the sages' debates over the interpretation of the Mishnah.

10 · THE BEGINNING OF CHRISTIANITY

Against the background of the Jewish wars on Rome, another process was also taking place. It was one whose impact would be felt far beyond the borders of Jewish history or of Eretz Yisrael. This was the rise of Christianity. Its story begins, as we have seen, during the time of Herod, at the start of the 1st century A.D. But it was only after the death of Jesus that Christianity began to take shape as a new religion.

THE EARLY CHRISTIANS

Although Jesus had a great deal of personal magnetism that attracted people to him, he did not set out to establish a new religion. On the contrary, he was born and died a Jew. Two men—Peter and Paul—were

that he was indeed the Messiah. It was from this belief that Christianity got its name. It comes from the Greek word *christos*, which means "messiah" or "savior." The apostles and disciples of Jesus saw no reason to continue to wait for another Messiah to appear, although some of them believed that Jesus would soon be resurrected and return to earth. Since one of the reasons for the Jewish revolts against Rome was the belief that the coming of the Messiah was at hand, these early Christians did not join in the rebellion. The repeated failure of the uprisings lent credence to their beliefs, and their numbers grew.

Most of what we know about the beginnings of Christianity comes from the New Testament. It is contained especially in the Acts of the Apostles

1. Jesus's disciples at the Last Supper, which took place on the festival of Passover just before Jesus's crucifixion, are depicted in this 6th century mosaic in a church in Ravenna, Italy.

2. "And when they came to the place which is called The Skull (Calvary), there they crucified him" (Luke 23:33). This gilded wall mosaic is in the Church of the Holy Sepulcher on the Via Dolorosa, the path Jesus walked to his crucifixion, in Jerusalem.

largely responsible for Christianity's development into a separate religion and for its rapid spread throughout the Roman empire.

After Jesus was crucified, his apostles became even more convinced

3. An aerial view of the Mount of Beatitudes, where Jesus is said to have preached the Sermon on the Mount.

4. Jesus and his disciples are carved in ivory on this Italian jewelry box from the 4th century.

5. Jesus, John the Baptist, and Paul appear in this mosaic in a church in Ravenna, Italy.

6. The route of Paul's journeys to spread Christianity.

which was probably written by Luke, who accompanied Paul on many of his journeys, and in the letters of Paul.

The first Christian community was established in Jerusalem. Immediately after the death of Jesus, one hundred and twenty of his followers gathered in Jerusalem and called themselves a "holy community."

They were soon joined by another 3,000 people, and together they lived a communal life which is described in Acts 2:37-42. In many ways, their way of life was similar to that of the members of the Qumran sect near the Dead Sea. The early Christians were clearly influenced by the beliefs of this sect. They shared their emphasis on rites of purification, their communal way of life, and most importantly their conviction in the imminent appearance of the Messiah. It is very likely that many of the members of the "holy community" of believers in Jesus had previously had some sort of contact with the Qumran sect.

Peter was the head of this community in Jerusalem. He came from the fishing village of Bethsaida on the shores of the Sea of Galilee. His Jewish name was Simon, but Jesus called him "Cephas," the Aramaic word for "rock." "Peter" is the Greek translation of that name. Peter was the first of the 12 apostles, Jesus's first disciples. He seems to have been the most talented and the best loved of them. After Jesus's death, Peter called on the Jews of Jerusalem to join

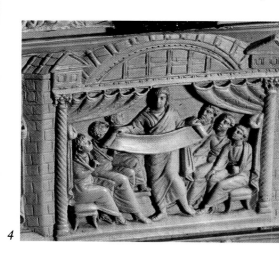

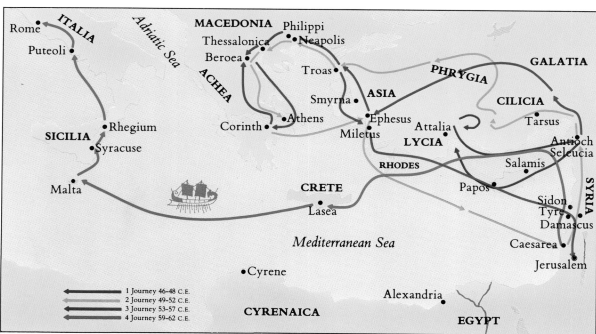

the believers in Jesus. Obviously, this turned the priests and sages of the Sanhedrin against him. There was now a serious breach between this Christian sect and the Sadducees and Pharisees. Under Peter's leadership, non-Jewish inhabitants of Eretz Yisrael—Samaritans, Greeks, and others—also became members of the community. According to Christian tradition, late in his life Peter journeyed to Rome and there he was arrested and crucified.

THE SPREAD OF CHRISTIANITY

Paul, like Peter, played a crucial role in shaping the new religion. He was largely responsible for the spread of Christianity throughout the Roman empire. Paul was born at the same time as Jesus. He was born to a Jewish family in the city of Tarsos in Cilicia (Turkey today) and was named Saul. By his own account, recorded in Acts, he was raised in Jerusalem and studied under the Pharisees. As a Pharisee, he was a violent persecutor of the early Christians, until one day "as he journeyed, he came near Damascus: and suddenly there shined round about him a light from heaven: And he fell to the earth, and heard a voice" (Acts 9:3-4). Here Jesus appeared to him in a vision and commanded him to spread his word throughout the world.

Peter was thus responsible for spreading Christianity among the Jews of Eretz Yisrael, while Paul—after his transforming experience on the road to Damascus—took it upon himself to bring the new religion to both the Jews and the non-Jews, or Gentiles, elsewhere in the empire.

The foundations for the widespread acceptance of Christianity had already been laid. Many people had converted to Judaism during the Hasmonean period, so that the belief in one God was no longer a strange and foreign idea. Jewish literature—the Hebrew Bible, the Apocrypha, the writings of the Jewish philosopher Philo of Alexandria, and other works—had

7. *A reconstruction of the site at Capernaum where Jesus and his disciples gathered. After leaving Nazareth, Jesus made his home in this town on the Sea of Galilee where he had many followers, among them Peter. According to Christian tradition, he performed several miracles and miraculous healings here.*

8. *A piece of cloth used by the Coptic Church in Ethiopia in the 5th century.*

9. *A mosaic at the Monastery of Lady Mary in Beit Shean from the 6th century.*

10. *John the Baptist in a 7th century icon from Crete in the Santa Katerina Monastery in Sinai.*

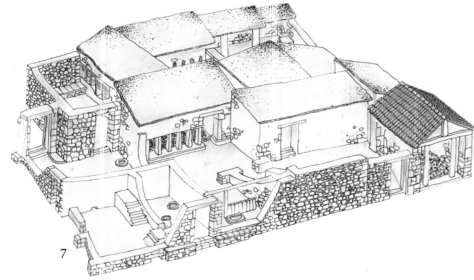

7

8

9

10

11

12

religious establishments in the Jewish communities throughout the empire.

Although Paul delivered most of his sermons in synagogues, his goal was to spread the belief in Jesus beyond the Jewish communities. He tried to convert pagans—those who worshipped many gods—to the new religion, too. Here is part of one of his sermons to the pagans: "We know that an idol is nothing in the world, and that there is none other God but one. For though there be that are called gods... to us there is but one God, the Father, of whom are all things, and we in him; and one Lord Jesus Christ, by whom are all things, and we by him" (1 Corinthians 8:4-6).

Paul was helped in this mission by one of the first Christian disciples, Barnabas. Barnabas had debated with Peter the question of whether non-Jewish converts to Christianity should be required to fulfill the commandments of Judaism, since Jesus had said that it was not his intention to change or abolish them.

Many pagans were reluctant to become Christians because of these commandments, particularly the requirement to undergo circumcision and the many restrictions regarding the food that could not be eaten. Paul, unlike Peter, held that the commandments need not be compulsory. In order to settle the question once and for all, he returned to Jerusalem. The members of the Christian community debated the issue and decided that Jews who joined them would be required to fulfill the commandments, while non-Jews would not. However, Gentiles could only be considered Christians if they "abstain from pollutions of idols, and from fornication, and from things strangled, and from blood" (Acts 15:20), in other words, if they refrained from offering sacrifices to idols, from prostitution, and from eating the meat of animals who had not been properly slaughtered or whose blood had not yet dried.

11. Here on the Hill of Temptation (Matthew 4:1) a monastery was built as early as the 4th century. The site, also known as the Mount of Quarantine, is near Jericho.

12. The lintel of a 4th century church. Note the encircled cross and the grapes and figs, typical fruits of the Land of Israel.

13. (On page 89) Nazareth, with the Basilica of the Annunciation in the foreground. Here, according to Christian tradition, Mary was told that she would give birth to the son of God.

been translated into Greek and was familiar to educated Hellenists. Moreover, Jews had settled in many places in the empire. Their communities, often rich and well-respected, were centers of monotheism. They journeyed frequently to Jerusalem, showing how important the city was to their belief. And the prophet Isaiah had said that the word of the Lord would go forth to all the nations from Jerusalem. So it is not surprising that when Paul, a Jewish student of the Pharisees from Jerusalem, preached his new version of Judaism, quite a number of Jews were persuaded by what he said, even though he was censured by the

THE BEGINNING OF
CHRISTIANITY

This decision was a turning point in the history of Christianity. It made it easier for the religion to spread rapidly among the Gentiles, but it was also the first true break between Christianity and Judaism. As more and more non-Jews converted to Christianity, the distinction between

13

14

the two religions grew greater.

Paul now increased his efforts to spread Christianity outside of Eretz Yisrael. He went on two missionary journeys (during the years 49-52 and 53-57), travelling from town to town throughout Syria, Asia Minor, the Aegean Islands, Greece, and Italy. In addition to preaching in public, Paul also wrote his sermons in Greek as letters to the various nations. These letters, or epistles, were the earliest sections of the New Testament to be written.

Paul's activities earned him many enemies among the Jews, the early Christians, and the Romans. He was imprisoned in Caesaria for two years and then taken to Rome in the year 60. There he was put to death.

During these years in the first century C.E., the literature of the New Testament was being written. After the death of Jesus, his disciples told of his life and beliefs in Hebrew, Aramaic, and Greek. But as Christianity spread, there was a growing need to write these stories down. Thus four of Jesus's early

15

disciples recorded their versions of his life, writing the books known as the Gospels. The language chosen was Greek, since it was the international language of the time. The first Gospel was most likely the one ascribed to Mark and was written in the years 66-68 C.E. during the Great Revolt of the Jews against Rome; the second, Matthew, in 80-90; the third, Luke, in 90-100; and the last, John, probably between 115 and 125. The Gospels are all in agreement about the major events, but like any story told by different people, they sometimes contradict each other. For this reason,

14. Christian communities in the Land of Israel in the 1st and 2nd centuries, and churches and synagogues up to the 3rd century.

15. "He (Jesus)...taking the five loaves and the two fish he looked up to heaven,...gave the loaves to the disciples, and the disciples gave them to the crowds" (Matthew 14:19). The mosaic floor of the Church of the Multiplication of the Loaves and the Fishes at Tabgha near the Sea of Galilee, the traditional site of this miracle.

16. *This silver star in the Grotto of the Nativity in Bethlehem marks the spot where Jesus is said to have been born.*

17. *An 18th century depiction of Santa Katerina in Sinai, one of the oldest monasteries in the region of Eretz Yisrael, probably established in the 4th century and still in operation.*

it is difficult to know the details of Jesus's life with any historical accuracy.

Around the year 200, the New Testament as we know it today, together with its first section—the Hebrew Bible, was officially recognized by the church as the Holy Scriptures. The Hebrew Bible now became known among Christians as the Old Testament.

Thus at the same time that Rabbi Judah ha-Nasi completed the *Mishnah*, the book of laws which has shaped the face of Judaism to this day, the Christian world also completed its sacred text, the New Testament which is the basis of Christian theology even today.

Both of these books, so different in nature, essentially grew out of the Hebrew Bible. And Eretz Yisrael, whose history we have told here, was the stage on which the events they relate were acted out.

THE BEGINNING OF
CHRISTIANITY

Glossary

Some of the terms which appear in this glossary are Hebrew. A phonetic pronunciation of these terms appears in parentheses.

Apocrypha
Greek for "hidden book." Writings considered sacred by various Jewish and Christian sects in the first centuries C.E., but which are not included in the Hebrew Bible or the New Testament. Some of them appear in the Septuagint. The name comes from the tradition that these ancient books were hidden away, and only discovered years later. Many of them are examples of pseudepigrapha.

Apostles
The 12 original disciples of Jesus.

Diaspora
Anywhere outside of Eretz Yisrael where Jews live.

Essenes
A Jewish sect in the Second Temple period which lived in communities near the Dead Sea. Their beliefs and communal way of life are described in the Dead Sea Scrolls.

Fertile Crescent
The area extending from the Persian Gulf, northward along the Euphrates and Tigris Rivers, and then westward and southward through the Land of Israel to the Nile River Valley.

Haggadah (ha-ga-dáh)
Hebrew for "telling" or "tale." A collection of blessings, prayers, commentaries, and hymns read at the Passover feast called the Seder.

Hanukkah (ha-noo-kháh)
Hebrew for "dedication." A Jewish holiday celebrated for eight days from the 25th of Kislev (the Jewish month usually falling in December) in honor of the victory of Judah Maccabee over the Greeks and the rededication of the Temple in 164 B.C.E. after it was cleansed of the defilement of Greek idolatry.

Hellenism
From *Hellas,* the Greek name for Greece. The Greek civilization which dominated the ancient world from the 4th century B.C.E to the 1st century C.E. This era is also known as the Hellenistic Period.

Hieroglyphics
Ancient Egyptian picture writing.

Icon
A holy picture, usually small and painted on wood, used in the religious rites of Eastern Christians.

Menorah (meh-no-ráh)
Hebrew for "lamp." A seven-branched candelabrum of gold, decorated with cups, knobs, and flowers. It was a ritual object in the Temple, and thus has been a Jewish symbol since ancient times.

Mishnah (mish-náh)
From the Hebrew for "learning" or "repetition." A book of Jewish law compiled by Judah ha-Nasi in 200 C.E. based on the accumulated interpretations and rulings of Jewish sages from ancient times.

Monotheism
The belief in one God, the single Creator and Ruler of the universe. Monotheism was a new idea introduced by the Jewish religion in Biblical times, and forms the basis of Christianity and Islam as well. The opposite of monotheism is polytheism, the belief in many gods ruling over the world.

Pehah (péh-háh)
A district governor appointed by the ancient Persian kings.

Pesach (péh-sakh)— Passover
A Jewish holiday celebrated for seven days in Israel and eight days in the Diaspora from the 15th of Nisan (the Jewish month falling in April or May) in commemoration of the Exodus from Egypt. It is also called the Festival of Spring and the Festival of Freedom. According to Christian tradition, Jesus's crucifixion and resurrection took place during Passover, and therefore the Easter holiday is celebrated at this time. In the first centuries C.E., Easter was the most important of the Christian holidays.

Pharisees
The largest Jewish sect during the Second Temple period which sought to maintain the purity of Jewish ritual. Most of its members came from the lower and middle classes. They disputed harshly with Jesus and fought the idea that he was the Messiah. Their major opponents were the Sadducees.

Polis (pl. Poleis)
A Greek city-state.

Pseudepigrapha
From the Greek for "fake book." A literary work in which the real author hides his identity and attributes the writing to a famous

historical figure. For example, *The Book of Adam and Eve,* written in the 1st century C.E., was claimed to have been written by Adam. Pseudepigraphic literature was common in the East in Greek and Roman times.

Resurrection
The rising of Jesus from the dead. According to Christian religion, Jesus rose from his grave three days after his death, an event commemorated by the Easter holiday.

Sadducees
A Jewish sect during the Second Temple period, supported mainly by the upper classes. Many of them held high positions in the Hasmonean kingdom, and under Roman rule the high priests were chosen from among them. Their major opponents were the Pharisees.

Sanhedrin (san-heh-dreén)
From the Greek for "council of elders." The supreme religious, judicial and legislative body of the Pharisees in Eretz Yisrael from the 1st century B.C.E. to the 4th century C.E.

Septuagint
From the Greek for "seventy." The earliest Greek translation of the Hebrew Bible. It was produced in Alexandria, Egypt in the 3rd century B.C.E. and also includes several of the apocryphal books. Today it serves as part of the Holy Scriptures of the Greek Orthodox Church. The name comes from the tradition whereby 70 sages each translated the Bible separately, but as the spirit of God was with them, all of the translations were identical.

Shavuot (shah-voo-óth)
Pentecost (the 50th day). A Jewish holiday celebrated 50 days after Passover, on which the first fruits were brought to the Temple. According to Jewish tradition, Moses received the Tablets of the Law on Mount Sinai on Shavuot. According to Christian tradition, the Holy Spirit revealed himself to Jesus's 12 apostles in Jerusalem on this day, and they began to speak in many tongues. As a result, Peter began to organize the first holy Christian community, which was the start of the universal church.

Talmud (tahl-moód)
From the Hebrew for "learning." A body of Jewish teaching in which the accumulated commentary and discussions of religious scholars on the Mishnah are collected. The Talmud contains religious laws and rulings in the fields of law, medicine, health, and agriculture, in addition to the beliefs and philosophy of Judaism.

Tanna, Tannaim (tah-náh, tah-nah-eém)
From the Aramaic for "to study." The sages of the 1st to 3rd centuries C.E. who took part in the creation of the Mishnah.

Temple
The central Jewish religious and national institution during the Biblical period. According to the Hebrew Bible, the original Tablets of the Law brought down from Mount Sinai by Moses resided in its inner sanctum, the Holy of Holies, which only the High Priest himself was allowed to enter once a year on the Day of Atonement. Three times a year, on the festivals of Succoth, The Feast of Tabernacles, Passover, and Shavuot, all of the Jews who were able gathered at the Temple in Jerusalem.
The First Temple was built by King Solomon in the 10th century B.C.E. and destroyed by Nebuchadnezzar, King of Babylon, in 587 B.C.E. The Second Temple was built by the exiles returning from Babylon in 515 B.C.E. and destroyed by the Romans in the year 70 C.E., during the Great Revolt.

Torah (toe-ráh)—Pentateuch
The first of the three sections of the Hebrew Bible consisting of five books: Genesis, Exodus, Leviticus, Numbers, and Deuteronomy. According to Jewish tradition, the Torah was given to Moses on Mount Sinai.

INDEX

Time Line of Biblical History

Eretz Yisrael		Egypt	Mesopotamia, Syria	Crete, Greece, Rome
3000 First towns		Development of hieroglyphic writing	Development of cuneiform writing	
2000 Patriarchs; Hyksos; Invention of alphabet	Israelites in Egypt	**1650-1560** Ruled by the Hyksos	**1792-1595** Hammurabi Dynasty	**1600** Start of Mycenae civilization in Greece
		1504-1450 Tuthmosis III		**1450** Destruction of Minoan Crete
		1350-1334 Akhebaten	**1350-612** Assyrian Kingdom	
		1290-1279 Seti I		
		1279-1212 Rameses II		
1230 Exodus from Egypt		**1212-1202** Merenptah		**1200** Trojan War
1200 Israelites conquer Canaan; Philistines in Canaan			**1114-1076** Tiglath-pileser I	
			Aram	
1150-1020 Period of the Judges				
1020-1004 Saul			Rezin	
1004-965 David				
965-928 Solomon		**945-924** Shishak		
Judah	**Israel**			
928-911 Rehoboam	**928-907** Jeroboam I			
911-908 Abijam	**907-906** Nadab			
908-867 Asa	**906-883** Baasha		Benhadad I	
	883-882 Elah, Zimri		**883-859** Ashurnasirpal II	
	882-871 Omri			
	873-852 Ahab		Benhadad II	
867-846 Jehoshaphat	**852-851** Ahaziah		**858-824** Shalmaneser III	
	851-842 Jehoram			
846-843 Jehoram	**842-814** Jehu			
843-842 Ahaziah				
842-836 Athaliah	**817-800** Jehoahaz		Benhadad III	**814** Founding of Carthage
836-798 Jehoash	**800-784** Jehoash		**809-783** Adad-nirari III	
798-769 Amaziah	**789-748** Jeroboam II			
769-733 Uzziah	**748** Zechariah			
758-743 Jotham (regent)	**748** Shallum		**745-727** Tiglath-Pileser III	**750** Homer
	747-737 Menahem			
743-733 Ahaz (regent)	**737-735** Pekahiah			
	735-733 Pekah			
	732-724 Hoshea			
733-727 Ahaz	**722** Fall of Samaria		**726-722** Shalmaneser V	**800-600** Founding of Rome; Greek expansion
727-698 Hezekiah	**720** Assyrian exile		**721-705** Sargon II	
701 Sennacherib Campaigns			**704-681** Sennacherib	
			680-669 Esaehaddon	
698-642 Manasseh				
641-640 Amon		**664-610** Psammetichus		
639-609 Josiah		**610-595** Necho		**621** Draco's laws
609 Battle of Megiddo; Jehoahaz			**668-627** Ashurbanipal	
608-598 Jehoiakim			**Babylon**	
597 Nebuchadnezzar campaigns; Jehoiakim exiled			**625-605** Nabopolassar	
			612 Fall of Nineveh	
595-586 Zedekiah			**605** Battle of Carchemish	**594** Solon's reforms
586 Destruction of Jerusalem and Babylonian exile			**604-562** Nebuchadnezzar	
585(?) Gedaliah murdered			**555-539** Nabunaid	

Eretz Yisrael	Egypt	Mesopotamia, Syria	Crete, Greece, Rome
		Persia	
538 Decree of Cyrus; Return to Zion		538 Cyrus conquers Babylon	
520–515 Building of Second Temple begun	525 Egypt conquered by Persia	529–522 Cambyses II	
		521–486 Darius II	510 Founding of Roman republic
		490 Battle of Marathon	
		485–465 Cyaxares (Ahasuerus)	480 Battle of Thermopylae
		464–424 Artaxerxes I	461–429 Age of Pericles
		423–405 Darius II	
	404 Egypt independent	404–359 Artaxerxes II	431–404 Peloponnesian War
		358–338 Artaxerxes III	399 Death of Socrates
	343 Conquered by Persia	335–331 Darius III	336 Alexander takes power
332 Eretz Yisrael conquered by Alexander the Great	332 Conquered by Alexander the Great	333 Battle of Issus	323 Death of Alexander
301 Start of Ptolemite rule	323–285 Ptolemy I		
	285–246 Ptolemy II Philadelphus; Septuagint		287–212 Archimedes
			264–241 First Punic War
	246–221 Ptolemy III Euergetes		
	221–203 Ptolemy IV Philopetor		218–202 Second Punic War
	203–181 Ptolemy V Epiphanes		
198 Start of Seleucid rule	181–146 Ptolemy VI Philometor	**Syria**	
168 Hasmonean revolt	168 Antiochus IV invades Egypt	175–164 Antiochus IV Epiphanes	
161 Fall of Nicanor; Alliance with Rome		162–152 Demetrius I	
160–142 Jonathan		152–145 Alexander Balas	
142–135 Simeon		145–138 Demetrius II; Antiochus VI Trypho	146 Fall of Carthage
134–104 John Hyrcanus I		138–129 Antiochus VII Sidetes	133 Start of rebellion against Rome
103–76 Alexander Yannai		129–125 Demetrius III	
76–67 Salome Alexandra			100–44 Julius Caesar
67–63 Judah Aristobulus II	69–30 Cleopatra VII		60 First Triumverate
63 Pompey in Eretz Yisrael		75–55 Gabinius, Roman procurator in Syria	
67, 63–40 John Hyrcanus II			31 B.C.E.–14 C.E. Augustus
40–37 Herod			14–37 Tiberius
C.E. 6–14 Judah, Samaria, & Edom become Roman provinces			
5–30 Jesus preaches			
26–36 Pontius Pilate procurator of Judea			
33 Jesus crucified; Peter & Paul active			
38–44 Agrippa I	C.E. 38 Attacks on Alexandrian Jews		37–41 Caius Caligula
44–66 Agrippa II			41–54 Claudius
66 Outbreak of revolt against Rome			54–68 Nero
67 Vespasian conquers the Galilee; Zealots control Jerusalem			64 Persecution of Christians
70 Destruction of Jerusalem			69–79 Vespasian
73 Fall of Masada; Judea becomes Roman province			79–81 Titus
			81–96 Domitian
106 Rome conquers Nabatean kingdom			98–117 Trajan
132–135 Bar Kokhba revolt	115–117 Jewish revolt against Trajan		117–138 Hadrian
135 Bethar falls; Aelia Capitolina founded			
140 Sanhedrin moves to Usha			138–161 Antoninus Pius
170 Sanhedrin moves to Bet She'arim			161–180 Marcus Aurelius
			180–192 Commodus
200 Sanhedrin moves to Zippori			193–211 Septimius Severus
210 Mishna completed by Judah ha-Nasi			211–217 Caracalla
		224 Founding of Sassanidae Dynasty	285–305 Diocletian
320 Judah II dies			337–361 Constantine II
324 Eretz Yisrael ruled by Byzantine Empire			340 Christianity declared official religion of Roman Empire